P9-BEE-653

BLOOD
SINISTER

BLOOD
SINISTER

Celia Rees

SCHOLASTIC

First published in the UK in 1996 by Scholastic Children's Books
An imprint of Scholastic Ltd
Euston House, 24 Eversholt Street
London, NW1 1DB, UK
Registered office: Westfield Road, Southam, Warwickshire, CV47 0RA
SCHOLASTIC and associated logos are trademarks and or registered trademarks of
Scholastic Inc.

This edition published in the UK by Scholastic Ltd, 2007
Text copyright © Celia Rees, 1996
The right of Celia Rees to be identified as the author of this work
has been asserted by her.

10 digit ISBN 1 407 10526 4
13 digit ISBN 978 1407 10526 0

A CIP catalogue record for this book is available from the British Library
All rights reserved
This book is sold subject to the condition that it shall not, by way of trade or
otherwise, be lent, hired out or otherwise circulated in any form of binding or cover other
than that in which it is published. No part of this publication may be reproduced, stored
in a retrieval system, or transmitted in any form or by any means (electronic, mechanical,
photocopying, recording or otherwise) without the prior written permission of
Scholastic Limited.

Printed in the UK by CPI Bookmarque, Croydon, CR0 4TD
Papers used by Scholastic Children's Books are made from wood grown in
sustainable forests.

3 5 7 9 10 8 6 4

This is a work of fiction. Names, characters, places, incidents and dialogues are
products of the author's imagination or are used fictitiously. Any resemblance to actual
people, living or dead, events or locales is entirely coincidental.

www.scholastic.co.uk/zone

Jo Poor

For Catrin

*Thanks to Myun-Sun, Yasue and Jovi (class of '95)
for help and advice about the Kang-shi*

PART ONE

"Take care," he said, "take care how you cut yourself.
It is more dangerous than you think…"

Count Dracula's advice to Jonathan Harker –
Dracula by Bram Stoker

1

Ellen Forrest was not ill. Not really. At least she didn't feel it most of the time, just tired, and everyone got tired. Everyone woke in the night, hot and sweaty one minute and chilly the next. It was a common experience. It happened to everybody now and again.

"Not as much as you. Not as much as it does to you," the little voice said in her head.

Lots of people got colds and sore throats, she argued back; loads felt fluey and achy. It was going to be a bad winter for it, they'd said so on the telly.

Rain drove against the windscreen as they swished through the wet November streets. There were not many pedestrians on the usually crowded London pavements. Those who had come out stumbled along, scowling and bent, coats wrapped around them. Ellen shivered, glad she was in the car.

"Are you all right, dear?" Her mother did not turn from her driving, but her voice came over sharp with concern. "Are you sure you're warm enough?" In the rear-view mirror, anxious eyes searched for hers. "There should be a shawl somewhere on the back seat, perhaps you should put it on…"

"I'm fine, Mum, honestly. Don't fuss."

"Well said." Her grandmother's lined faced creased further as she smiled from the front passenger seat. Her blue eyes, magnified by thick spectacle lenses, flashed a powerful message of support to Ellen. "Leave the child alone, Stella. She's sixteen, not a toddler. She's swaddled up enough as it is."

"But the specialist said…"

Ellen sighed and leaned back in her seat. Her mother had put on her special "doctor" voice and was going through it all again for the hundredth time. The symptoms: what they thought it was, what they thought it might be, what they definitely knew it wasn't. And, Ellen suppressed a shudder, then there were the tests. Hollow needles, spurting liquid. Long shiny tubes, ruby red with blood, snaking in or out of her. *This won't hurt a bit*. But it always did. Ellen stared out at the slick wet streets, trying not to feel sick.

"The fact of the matter is," Edith Baxter said, cutting into her granddaughter's medical history, "they haven't got a clue what's wrong with her." Her old arthritic hand groped the back of her seat, feeling for Ellen's. "That's why she's here. Meanwhile, she's not an invalid and I, for one, don't intend to treat her as such. Ah, we're here."

The car swung into the short drive. Shrubs and tall trees grew close up, shutting the tall Victorian house off from the street. It showed no welcoming light and in the late afternoon, as day edged towards night, it looked gloomy, forbidding, even creepy.

Not as creepy as what's across the road, Ellen told herself, deliberately not looking in that direction. You couldn't see much really, not from street level, just a high wall topped with railings. It curved the whole length of the road, marking the boundary of the oldest part of one of the biggest cemeteries in London. Almost directly opposite her grandmother's house was one of the gates. STRICTLY NO ADMITTANCE a peeling notice said, but they were no longer in use. They hadn't been opened in thirty years. Saplings had grown up, weaving through the rusting bars, adding their living strength to the chains and padlocks. Everything was so overgrown it looked like a forest; you couldn't even see the path behind.

From above, from the top of Gran's house, it was possible to see more. The dirty white marble of crumbling mausoleums gleamed through the canopy of leaves and, here and there, fallen granite columns and broken stone angels showed in gaps in the greenery. Some of the damage had been done by vandals, but mostly it was the work of trees, now huge, full grown, thrusting root and trunk through bone, wood and stone.

It was a wild place, strange and dangerous. Public notices barred access for good reason. There were no real pathways left, it was easy to get lost, and the ground was honeycombed with crumbling vaults and passages. In some places huge holes yawned under a thin disguise of grass and brambles. In others one step was enough to break through rotten brick to a pit deep enough to hide a house. Besides, even on the brightest day, it was a place of shadows. Crowded on all sides by streets and houses, it remained an island of eerie silence.

She had never explored the tangled interior, only seen it

from the attic. Andy had. She hadn't seen him for years; but when she was a kid and had come to stay, he'd always been round to play. He knew the cemetery like the back of his hand, or said he did. One day, he'd dared them to go in there with him. Ellen and her sister, Karen, had said, "No way!" so he'd gone on his own. That was morning and he didn't emerge until late afternoon. He'd gone straight home, pale and subdued, and had never said a word about what, if anything, had taken place.

"Can you manage?"

Her mother had come round to open the car door and help her out.

"Of course I can! I told you before, Mum, don't fuss over me. I'm not a baby!"

But even as she said the words she felt the strength draining from her, leaving her legs useless and wobbly. Despite herself, she had to lean against the car to gather her strength for the walk to the steps. Because she was sick. She was very sick. She could feel it deep down inside when it overtook her like this, see it in her mother's anxious stare and her grandmother's look of sudden sadness.

A row of holly bushes, dark and bulky, cut the view of the cemetery down to patches of brick. It looked like any other wall, you'd never guess what lay behind it. Ellen found herself wondering what exactly had happened in there. What kind of experience could it be to affect a boy like Andy and scare him witless?

2

The next day she felt fine again. Even had an appetite. Her grandmother brought her breakfast in bed and she ate it all, even the boiled egg which wasn't exactly a favourite. It was like that, this mystery sickness, it came and went.

There was something wrong with her but no one could discover what. Something wrong with her blood, that was all they knew, or all they were saying to her. Their manner had changed over the year since it had all started. The cheery "We'll soon have you right as rain, young lady" remarks had gradually faltered, reassuring smiles had turned into puzzled shakes of the head. Now, if they talked at all, it was to each other, or to her father and mother, always just out of earshot, out in the corridor, or in Sister's office. Her case had been referred to one of the big London teaching hospitals. Mum had gone back, leaving her at Gran's. It was nearer to the specialist consultants and their dedicated unit. All she had to do was wait to be called in so they could get another round of tests started.

"I'm going out now, dear. Do you want anything from the shops?"

Gran came in already dressed for the raw weather outside. The purples and greens of her tweed coat matched her soft-brimmed hat; a mauve angora scarf pinned at her throat with an amethyst brooch completed the ensemble.

"*Mizz* or *Just Seventeen*," Ellen said from the bed. "They are magazines," she added.

"I know that. I don't live in a time warp," her grandmother replied. "I'm quite aware that newsagents stock other items besides *Woman's Journal* and *Homes and Gardens*!"

Ellen smiled. She quite enjoyed Gran's sharp tongue.

"Well, I'm off," Edith Baxter said, pulling on fur-lined gloves. "No need to lie about feeling sorry for yourself. Besides the television, there's plenty of books to read. Annie is downstairs if you need anything. I'll see you later."

Ellen dressed and sat on the side of the bed wondering what to do. Annie's singing filtered up the stairs from the bottom of the house. She didn't really want to go down and make polite conversation. Gran's home help knew why she was there and was bound to cluck over her and ask questions. Instead, she left her room and headed in the opposite direction, up the little flight of stairs which led to the attic.

She had been up there before, of course, with Andy. Karen, her sister, never came up. She was younger than

Ellen and scaredy. One year they had made up some story about a ghost to stop her tagging along with them. Something about a headless body in a trunk and "presences". Karen had been so terrified she wouldn't even sleep on the floor below, had made Ellen swap beds. She smiled. Karen really could drive her round the bend but suddenly she missed her sister.

The eaves sloped inwards in an inverted V, but the attics were proper rooms, not a trapdoor in the ceiling like at home. They were packed floor to ceiling with all kinds of junk but there was still plenty of space to move about. Ellen looked around, trying to ward off the sense of disappointment creeping through her. She used to look forward to this, exploring, looking for secrets. Now everything appeared to be exactly what it actually was, stuff that had been banished from the rest of the house: chairs with wonky legs; a leather settee with horsehair poking out; things belonging to Grandad, fishing rods and cricket bats, ancient tennis racquets with broken catgut strings, piled up in corners. It was like the old wardrobe. She and Andy had climbed in, expecting to find a route to a magic world, but there was no way out, just a couple of hairy old sports coats swinging in front of a solid plywood back.

They had practically pulled the old desk apart looking for secret compartments and hidden springs, but had found nothing but old bills and broken pencils.

She sat down in a deeply sagging armchair, her feet on the box in front of her. It wasn't a box, in fact, it was a trunk, green tin with leather hinges. She leaned forward, examining it more carefully. She didn't remember it from the last time, someone must have been moving things. It was not big enough to hide a body in – except a very small one. The trunk was a bit the worse for wear, the pale pea-green paint badly scratched, the top all bashed. It had letters on the side, faintly stencilled in what must have been gold: E.L.M.

Secured with a sturdy padlock, iron and brass, it was rather smart. No key, but then there wouldn't be. Ellen leaned over and tried the hasp. It was secured by rust, apart from anything else, but that didn't matter because the whole lid was loose. The leather of the hinges had perished, nearly rotted through; it looked like mice had been nibbling away at them, too. She retrieved an old broken penknife from the desk drawer. Using it like a saw, she released the straps and flipped open the box.

At first she thought it was just like the desk, full of an unrewarding jumble of old papers, but these did appear to be slightly more interesting. There were photographs and newspaper cuttings among what looked like personal letters, and something else. Ellen pushed the sheets of paper to one side.

A book jutted out, and beneath that another, going down like steps to the bottom of the trunk. She took one out and looked at the cover. It was about the same size as an exercise book, but stiffly bound in dark blue, with a leather back and re-inforced corners. LOG BOOK was stamped in gold letters on the front and the pages were edged in thin wavy bands of rainbow colours. Ellen, who had never kept a diary for more than a few days, could feel the pull of the book, the desire to have it to write in and fill with words of your own.

She opened the cover, aware of its age, careful of the creaking back, not wanting to hurt it.

Ellen Laidlaw
HER BOOK
1878
To keep this safe from prying eyes
Cursed be he who looks inside

A square of white paper was gummed on to the marbled inside cover. The verse was accompanied by a little devil drawn in red ink, complete with a horrible grimacing face, pitchfork and nest of flames licking all around him. The handwriting was copperplate, small and incredibly neat, sloping to the right with loops above and below the lines. Executed well over a hundred years ago, Indian ink had kept the letters fresh and black.

Ellen looked at the page, her heart beating fast. This was a discovery. There might be secrets here. The writer, Ellen Laidlaw, became Ellen Laidlaw-Macmillan. She was famous and Ellen's great-great-grandmother. Ellen knew about her. A pioneering woman doctor. They shared the same name, she'd been told about that and, anyway, she had once done a project on her. 1878. She would have been young when she wrote this, about the same age as Ellen was now. This must be her diary.

A sound made Ellen look up. It was only rain, sharp on the window pane. Nevertheless, she put the book down and went to look out. The weather was atrocious, there was no one about. Then she noticed a man walking down the road, close against the high cemetery wall. He was wearing a long black overcoat, collar up against the wind. His face was turned away, and on his head, pulled right down, he wore a broad-brimmed hat. When he got to the overgrown gate, he stopped and peered in. His gloved hand reached forward to test the huge rusting chain, tugging at the hanging padlock. Then he turned round.

His face, white beneath the black fedora, looked straight up at her. There was no way that he could see her, he was at least thirty metres away and she was right at the top of a three-storey house. Even so, Ellen felt their eyes meet. It was as though his eyes were searching for hers, focusing finer and finer, like high-powered binoculars. As she watched, the rain began to turn to sleet.

Instinctively, she dropped out of his reach, staying crouched down as little balls of ice began to skitter against the window above her. The sound they made was like pebbles thrown up at the glass or the scratching of fingernails.

Moments later, telling herself not to be so stupid, she peered over the sill. But he had gone. There was no sign of him anywhere. She took in the whole length of the long curving street. He had simply vanished.

3

Ellen carried a couple of the books downstairs but, just as she opened the first volume, her grandmother returned from her shopping trip. It was much later on in the evening before she could return to the privacy of her room and start to read.

It began:

13th January, 1878

I have never kept a diary, why do I start now? Why have I waited until my sixteenth year? And why today of all days? Some of the girls at the school have begun journals, but I do not choose to follow them, or start on the first day of the new year as they did: Dear Diary. All I know is this. On my way home today I visited the stationers', to buy this and that for the new school term, and instead of nibs and pens and such, I found myself reaching for a fine notebook, large and leather-bound. I had resolved to keep a diary before the shop assistant had wrapped my purchase.

I will write, each day, what happens to me. The diary will be my companion, like someone my own age in whom I can confide. I seldom speak to the other girls at school. I have no friends. To know friendship, and then have it withdrawn bit by bit, as it was in the last place we lived, is most cruel. Prejudiced provincials, unable to appreciate the importance of his work, Father said. London will be different. Perhaps so. But I cannot risk it.

I am afraid even to tell them where I live. When we leave the High School, they go north and west, while I go south and east. Papa's work compels us to live in one of the poorest areas of the capital. He is a doctor. Anthony Laidlaw M.D., specialist in diseases of the brain, and of the blood, an authority. But he believes that medicine should be freely available to anyone, rich and poor. He must be in the place where there is most need. It is his duty. I know that the other girls at school would not understand. I have seen them turn pale and wrinkle their noses in horror and disgust at the very name of the district where we live. And as for our house? I have heard them invite each other to tea, but that would be impossible for me.

It is a hospital. The foundation goes back to Tudor times, but some parts are much older. Along certain corridors, where some of Father's more unfortunate patients gibber and howl their distress, brick walls give way to stone, opening into areas more resembling chapel or crypt than a place to nurse the sick. The building was deserted, half fallen into ruin, when Father came to own it. The very name filled the local population with *superstitious dread. My father has changed that! Now it equals any hospital in the country.*

Our quarters have been made pleasant enough, but I could not bring school fellows here, even if their parents would allow them to accompany me. The tops of the high walls glitter with shards of broken glass and the buildings have a grim aspect, even in bright sunlight.

Tom has just come in. Papa bids me change and go downstairs to the drawing room. We have guests this evening. Strange. We entertain seldom and usually Papa warns me. I have no mama, I am expected to take her place if we have company.

I ask Tom who they are, but he does not know.

"Foreign types." He shrugs and grins. "Mrs Dover's on her way up, so you'd better stop scribbling and get out of that inky pinafore."

I like Tom. We get on very well, even if he does tease me. Tom Macmillan is my father's assistant. He is not a doctor – yet. He is tall, with fair, curly hair. His face? More likeable than handsome, but I find it pleasant enough. He has blue eyes, or are they grey? I will have to pay attention to such details if I am to keep a diary. Blue, I see as they smile into mine. They are kind, amused, surrounded by laughter lines. He is my friend. Perhaps more than that.

Some of the girls at school whisper and giggle about the young men they meet at dances and soirées. They all seem to have legions of admirers. I am in no position to join in with this talk. Tom is the only young man I know, but I wouldn't swap him for any number of their Edwards, Williams and Henrys. They seem shallow, silly, chattering about nothing. Tom and I talk long and hard about many subjects. We don't always agree, but that just adds a little spice, as Cook would say. We spend as much time together as we can, but Tom is kept very busy. He divides his hours between here and the London Hospital where he is completing his training.

As for anything else – I don't moon about him, like the girls at school, and if it is love, it is not as they describe it, but I feel that he is dear to me and I look forward to his company. If he meets me, I hardly notice the journey home. If he does not, the walk seems very slow and tedious. I am not sure, as yet, what Tom's feelings are. Eloquent on so many subjects, he is very shy about things like that. Once or twice he has seemed about to say something but his tongue just gets tied in knots. It is not my place to speak, I might be mistaken, but somehow I don't think so. The other night, on our way home, he took my hand and I did not take it back. The girls at school would find this very tame, but my heart beat faster than our footsteps as we walked along the pavement. I don't care for their opinion. I must learn to trust my own emotions, not their judgement.

I can hear Mrs Dover, our housekeeper, outside the door. I do not want her to know about my diary. She would be sure to read it and I blush to think of her seeing what I have just written. It is time to put the pen aside, pick up the hairbrush and begin to prepare for this evening. I wonder who these people can be? They must be important if she's been sent to help me get ready.

14th January, 1878

It is after midnight but I am still wide awake. I will write *until sleep comes to me. If I go over to the window, I can see well enough.*

I put down my pen just as Mrs Dover was about to come in. She has looked after me since I was a tiny child. I love her dearly, but her temper is uncertain. Loving kindness can change with the wind to chilly disapproval. The unexpected unsettles her, so this evening she was at her most fussy. She shook out nearly every dress I possess and forced me into one I particularly hate. It is cut too low, a deep rose-pink frilly thing that does not become me. She then attacked my hair with unbridled ferocity.

When she had finished, she softened a little and made me get out Mama's jewellery. It is mine but I rarely wear any of it. Dover took out a necklace, set with blood-red garnets and milky opals and, removing my plain silver cross, clasped it around my neck. Then, turning me round to face the mirror, she pronounced, "You'll do."

This is high praise from Dover.

"Don't just stand there staring at yourself, Miss Vanity!" she said, as she left the room.

I considered this unfair as I rarely take an interest in my own appearance but, I must confess, I did stay for a few moments, studying my reflection. In the soft lamplight my hair shone like spun gold, thanks to Dover's vigorous brushing. It was swept up, away from my face. Together with the garnets and the low-cut dress, it made me look older than my actual years, like someone else. My eyes strayed to the wall at the side of my bed and the portrait there. My heart skipped a beat. It has been said many times, but I never believed it before. I look just like my mother!

I glanced back to the mirror, intrigued by the

difference I saw – and the likeness. Colour brushed each
cheek, and my eyes seemed to have changed from their
usual dull clerical grey to a smoky, almost purple,
darkness.

Ellen stopped reading and got up. She turned the bedside
lamp round to get a better light and went over to the
dressing-table. Her hair was dark, like her father's, and
not exactly shiny. It looked dull, wispy, the ends split and
brittle. Clerical grey though… Ellen studied her own eyes;
that was an excellent description. She wandered back to
the bed. There were photographs in the trunk; maybe
there was one of her ancestor taken at the time she was
describing. Suddenly she was even more intrigued by this
other Ellen. She picked up the diary again. She'd left her
standing in the hall. There was just time to read a bit
before she had to get ready for bed.

My new-found confidence seemed to drain out through
the soles of my feet as I stood before the drawing room's
great mahogany doors. I would have bolted away if
Dover had not come up behind and pushed me.
"Go on!" she hissed. "What are you doing, dithering
about?"
Papa was standing by the fireplace, talking to a
woman. They were laughing and drinking wine – the cut
glass made it shine like jewels in the firelight. Papa turned
and smiled as I came in. He looked very handsome in
evening dress; his dark curling hair is only just starting to
silver and his moustache and little pointed beard are as
black as ever. The lady smiled also and came hurrying
towards me with much rustling of black satin. A large,

handsome woman, her dress was cut low and she displayed a quantity of jewellery against clear creamy skin: diamonds, and large square-cut sapphires matched to the unusual colour of her eyes. They were not black, as I had thought at first, but a dark, clouded blue. Her hair was elaborately dressed, with a lustrous greeny shine like a raven's back.

When she spoke, her voice was rich and deep – her accent making her English, though excellent, sound exotic.

"My dear Anton, is this your daughter? You did not tell me she was so beautiful. Come, my dear, over here, let me look at you." She took my wrist in a strong grip and propelled me into the light. "Yes, yes! To the life! She is Isobel!"

As she said this, her fingers, heavily ringed and rather fat, caressed my cheek from near my ear to the point of my chin. Her hand was icy cold. Either her touch, or the reference to my mother, made me instinctively flinch away from her. Luckily, she took this for modesty.

"You English are so shy. Why so terrified of compliments, my little one? Such purity! Such loveliness!"

At this she pinched my cheek, a sensation as unpleasant as the one that went before it. There was something greedy and devouring about the expression in her eyes, almost frightening. I did not know what to do. Fortunately, Papa came to my rescue.

"Elizabetta! You are frightening the life out of her – leave the poor girl alone. Come here, my poppet, let me introduce you properly." I went to my father's side, glad of his protecting arm around my shoulders. "Ellen, may I introduce the Countess Elizabeth Vardalek and her kinsman, Count Fransz Szekelys. Very old, very dear friends…"

At the last name I turned, unaware that there was anyone else in the room besides my father and this woman. A young man sat, half-reclining, on the couch.

"Forgive me that I do not get up…" he said, leaving the rest of the sentence dangling.

He was very pale. White to the point of transparency. You could see veins under the skin. I wondered, as I went to greet him, if this was the origin of the term blue-blooded aristocracy. His hair was dark, thick, and brushed straight back. When I got close, I saw that it was very deep auburn. High cheek-bones and fine features gave his face a delicate, nearly Oriental cast. His full lips and finely moulded chin gave him an almost feminine beauty.

I held out my hand to shake his, but he took it and pressed it to his mouth. His lips were warm, his hands as cold as his cousin's. He had elongated, bony fingers; long nails for a man, and sharp — one of them grazed my palm. He looked up into my eyes and smiled. His own were also a most peculiar shade. Dark green, with flecks of gold, brown and red, which seemed to radiate from the centre of the iris. I found myself looking right into them, puzzling what the colours and the patterns might be, knowing I was staring, unable to break away, until the room seemed to recede from me. He turned my hand, touching the underside to his lips.

"Our ways are not your ways." His smile widened to show white teeth, sharp and oddly shaped. His voice, heavily accented, seemed to purr in my ears. "I embarrass you also. Forgive me."

To my intense relief, Marie, the maid, arrived to announce that dinner was served.

The Count ate little and drank less; the Countess more than made up for her kinsman's lack of appetite. It appears that she and my father are old acquaintances, although he has never mentioned her before in my hearing. They met in the German spa of Baden-Baden. This is where she must have met my mother. My parents lived there for a time before I was born, he practising as a doctor, she searching for a cure.

"Your father is the most wonderful doctor, my dear. And your mother, so beautiful!" She threw up her plump arms in a gesture of despair. "And so young!" She shook her head, setting her diamonds tinkling. "Such a shame, such a pity. Poor Anton!"

She cast her large dark eyes in my father's direction. I did not like the way she shortened his name, or the way she looked at him. Her references to times I knew nothing of, relationships I knew nothing about, the way she hinted that she and the Count had shared a part of my father's life I could not even guess at, all this made me feel strange, uncomfortable. I was relieved when the meal was over and I could absent myself.

I bade them good-night and assumed they would be leaving together but, when I opened the curtains just now, I saw that only she got into the waiting carriage. The Count must still be here. I crept out on to the landing a few moments ago and heard male voices coming from Papa's study and smelt cigar smoke, distant but distinct.

I must stop. I have written myself to the point of exhaustion and have discovered a tiny cut on my hand which is beginning to bleed, smearing the page as I write.

I have no idea where I got it. It is like a cut from a razor, or paper, clean-edged but sore. But I will not bother Papa with such a trivial wound. I will deal with it myself in the morning.

"Ellen, my dear. I think it's time you turned off your light."

"Yeah." Ellen put the diary down. "I'm going to. Night, Gran."

"Good-night."

She tucked the diary under her bed. There was a handy space there. She couldn't keep trooping up and down to the attic. She'd go and fetch the whole trunk, bring it down to her room tomorrow.

4

The box was heavier than she thought. Or she was weaker. Ellen collapsed back on the old settee, her arms shaking and her face glazed with sweat. The trunk sat where it was. Some kind of sixth sense had told her not to share the discovery with her grandmother, so how was she going to get it downstairs? She was the kind of person who, as soon as she couldn't have something, wanted it all the more. Damn it!

"Ellen – there's a visitor for you. Ellen? Where are you?"

Gran's voice, faint at first, grew louder as she climbed the stairs. Ellen stood up and went over to the little door.

"I'm up here. I'll be down in a minute."

A visitor. For her. Who on earth could that be? She looked down at her ratty old jeans and sweatshirt. Her hair probably looked worse than it had the night before. She hoped it was no one important.

"I'll leave you two," her gran said, and made a diplomatic exit.

It was a cold day. Andy's coat held the sharp, frosty smell of outdoors. He looked completely different from the boy she'd last seen years ago. He was about two feet taller for a start and his voice, when he said hello, was much deeper. His face had changed as well, the round shape had gone and so had the fresh complexion. His features were clearly defined and would stay the same through his adult life. A rather broad nose, wide cheek bones and a strong jaw line. His mouth still turned up at the corners, but the effect now was charming rather than cheeky. His hair was cut in a recognizable style, instead of looking like his mother had been at it with the bacon scissors. It was still dark brown, but shiny and soft, freshly washed. It flopped over blue eyes which had stayed the same, as lazy and mischievous as the first time she'd met him.

"You've changed," she said, almost accusing him.

"So have you," he replied. "It's called hormones."

He kept his smile wide, hoping he could hide the shock he felt. Her grandmother had warned him but he couldn't believe how thin she was. Her grey eyes were circled with shadowy rings and looked huge in a face that was all planes and angles. The shiny cap of hair had grown long, straggling on to her shoulders, and her hand was thin and cold – he could feel every bone as he took it gently into his.

"How are you?" he asked.

"I'm fine."

"You look great!"

"I do not. I look like…"

"OK." He laughed. "I've seen you looking better. But your gran said … your illness… Do they know?"

"No, they don't. And I don't want to talk about it."

She shut her eyes. The lids showed a tracery of blue veins.

"All right. What shall we talk about then?"

Ellen opened her eyes again.

"Tell you what. You know the attic? We used to explore there when we were kids?"

He nodded.

"Can you do me a favour?"

"Where do you want it?"

He had picked it up like it was nothing. He was standing in her bedroom doorway now, large hands clamped either side, the trunk clutched to his chest.

"Over here. Under the bed."

He dropped the box to the floor and shoved it into its new home.

"Aren't you going to tell me what's in there, then?" he said, dusting his hands off.

She shrugged. "Just old family stuff. Thought I'd go through it. There's not much else to do."

"Yeah. Right. Look. I can come round. Any time. Keep you company…"

"There's really no need." She was trying to keep the bitterness out of her voice, but wasn't succeeding very well. "I'm sure you've got millions of better things to do than visiting invalids."

"I haven't, honestly. Wheel your chair round the park? You just have to ask."

"I'm not that bad yet."

Despite herself, Ellen began to laugh.

"That's better." He grinned. "Seriously – I'd be happy to

come by, often as you like. But," he looked at his watch, "right now, I've got to run or I'll be late."

"For what?"

"College. Other side of the Cem. Can I drop by later?"

"Yes. If you want."

"See you then."

She watched from the window as he ran down the road. To her surprise she found herself wanting him to drop by later, wanting it quite a lot.

Having a bath and washing her hair, sorting out decent clothes from the ones her mother had packed for her, it all helped to fill the empty day. She even sat at the mirror and started putting on make-up. It was quite a long time since she'd done that and it made her feel heaps better.

"You look very pretty, dear," her grandmother said as she came in to the room. "That was Andrew on the phone. He can't come over, I'm afraid, too much work at the moment. He'll try to make it another day."

"That's OK. I'm feeling a bit tired, anyway," Ellen replied, without looking round.

"You have a little rest and I'll call you when supper's ready."

Ellen lay down. Her hand groped under the bed until she found the diary.

15th January, 1878

12:30p.m. I'm writing this at school during dinner recess. The other girls have gone out to play, or wander round the grounds in little groups, but I'm on duty in the library which is empty. This suits me. No one invites me to be with them and I do not wish for company.

The Count is definitely staying. When I came down for breakfast, Cook was complaining. Papa was nowhere to be seen so I ate in the kitchen. Porridge. It is supposed to be good for me. I hate it.

"He won't eat that," Cook said. "Bits of toast. That's all he wants. Not even butter on it. Foreigners!"

Marie and Mrs Dover nodded in agreement. They share Cook's suspicion of anyone who comes from anywhere east of Greenwich.

The Count's needs were to be catered for by us, not the hospital kitchen. Cook is less than happy about it.

"Seen that servant of his?" Cook went on, continuing her tirade. "Like a man mountain. Wanted a piece of steak big as my head. Hardly seen the pan. He wanted it all bloody."

Cook's shudder was echoed by Marie but she was soon absorbed again in the Police Gazette.

"Seen this, Cook?"

"What's that, my dear?"

Cook looked over her shoulder and they became involved in a discussion about a particularly grisly murder. I wanted to have a look but Dover's nose twitched and I was packed off to school. Marie tells her it's only a bit of fun but Dover disapproves of the Police Gazette. *She thinks it a bad influence. Sometimes Marie leaves it in my room. By accident.*

5:30p.m. I am fatigued and thoroughly out of temper. Tom walked me home from school, but any pleasure I felt died when he told me this would be the last occasion for quite some while. He has volunteered for night duty at the hospital. When I ask why he replies that he has to gain clinical experience if he is to qualify and he has also promised to tutor his friend Caspar. Caspar works there as a night porter. He is Hungarian and was studying medicine in Vienna when his political activities came to the notice of the authorities and he was forced to leave the country. He arrived in Britain penniless, without a word of the language, but he hopes one day to continue his studies here. It is so like Tom to help other people, and I know I'm being unreasonable, but I can't help feeling neglected. He asked me what the matter was but I did not reply and we walked the rest of the way home in silence.

Perhaps he has no feelings towards me, or no more than brother has for sister. Perhaps I have been deluding myself. When I think that, my cheeks grow hot.

I just want to be left alone but Papa insists I dress again for dinner. I protest that I am tired, I have homework to do, but he dismisses this with a wave of his hand. I have to be there, to be on show. Dinner will be proper and formal now we have a guest.

"What guest?" I ask.

The Count. He is to be with us for some time as guest and patient combined.

Later – dinner was tedious. I excused myself as soon as possible.

Papa has just been to my room. He says to me that the Count has requested that I keep him company.

"In what way?" I enquired.

"Talk to him. Play chess with him." Papa was swaying slightly, smelling of brandy and cigars. He stroked his beard, smiling at me. "He wants to improve his English."

The mood I was in led me to object. I have school work, I said, and I don't want to spend my evenings trying to converse with a stranger. Anyway, it wouldn't be right for me to be there alone, without a chaperone. My refusal angered Papa. His excellent mood began to evaporate.

"The Count is an old and valued friend," he said, curt and clipped. "I owe him, and his cousin, a very great debt, and so do you. When Isobel, your mother, became so very ill, I was at my wits' end. With few patients, in a strange land," his voice cracked, "near collapse myself. I do not know what I would have done..." A muscle in his cheek jumped. "They took over her care, they were generous to a fault, unstinting with money, time and help. Nothing was too much trouble. It was hopeless in the end. All to no avail. She was lost," he paused, passing a hand over his face, as if to wipe the memory from his eyes, then his gaze came back to me, "but you were saved. Now I have been given the chance to repay all their help, all their kindness.

"The Count's condition was manageable at one time, but over the last few years it has become much more serious. He has come to me seeking a cure. I cannot promise that, but I think I can offer him hope." He looked down at me, brows arrowing into a frown. "He may die. He may be dying now. Would you deny him what little diversion your company might offer? Because of school work? For lack of a suitable chaperone? Ivan, his man servant, would be there in any case." His tone dripped sarcasm and contempt. "Think what you are saying, Ellen."

He has left me to consider. I could ask Tom about what I should do but, of course, he isn't here. I have a feeling he would advise me against, perhaps even ask to take my place.

16th January, 1878

7:30a.m. I shall agree to do as Papa wishes. After a night's sleep, my objections begin to seem petty and selfish, even to me. Besides that, I do not know how long I can endure Papa's disapproval.

Ellen flipped over to a blank page and then a lot of doodles and a couple of false starts. After an impressive opening, this was beginning to resemble her own diary-keeping. The next solid entry was dated 6th February – almost a month later.

6th February, 1878

The Count is still here but he is grievously ill. Papa is very, very concerned about him. I am as well. That is why I have taken up my diary again; I need someone to talk to.

I have just looked back at my last entries. Papa was right, as usual. The concerns I expressed were groundless. Visiting the Count was not the ordeal I thought it would be. Tom disapproved, as I sensed he would, but, then again, he did volunteer to absent himself from my company. Fransz has proved to be a different but, nevertheless, a charming and fascinating companion. I now look forward to my visits and have seen him nearly every day – which makes his deterioration over the last week or so all the more obvious and all the more distressing.

The night of my first visit, my heart felt full of lead. His apartment is far from ours, down in the depths of the old part of the building. I walked as slowly as possible, hoping it would take a long time to get there. I was surprised that he had been put there instead of in the house as our guest. I said as much to Papa, who replied that it was at his own request and scolded me for dawdling. He was still annoyed with me. Even though I had agreed to do as he asked, there was still bad feeling between us and that made me unhappy; knowing where we were going did not help my mood either. I rarely visit this area. It little resembles the airy wards and well-lit corridors of the upper part of the building.

It is more like a prison than a hospital. Only the most hopeless and difficult patients are kept down here. The attendants are all big burly men who look more like gaolers than nurses. The walls are bare brick. A row of pegs holds the straitjackets used to subdue the patients and everywhere there is the jangle of keys and the slamming of iron on stone as each successive gate is unlocked to allow you through and then locked behind you. The terrible shrieks from some of the cells can be alarming and frightening, but I find the pathetic whimpering and little dry whispers coming from behind certain of the studded iron doors far more distressing. I try to appear indifferent, I am the Doctor's daughter, but being down there makes me nervous.

When we got to the Count's apartments, I was pleasantly surprised. He is living in the oldest part of the building of all. The room is in the shape of an octagon, the walls are of stone. Pillars support the roof, like in a crypt, and some of them are carved with strange designs.

Father told me that scholars believe it to have been built by the Knights Templar for their arcane occult rituals, but no one knows that for sure.

Whatever its original purpose, the room had been transformed from the last time I'd seen it. The Countess has taken a house in Highgate for the duration of her cousin's treatment and she must have scoured every shop in London to provide him with the most comfortable and sumptuous of furnishings. Oil lamps and candles compensate for the lack of natural light and cast a suffused glow over everything. Richly patterned carpets adorn the floors and walls, a heavy brocaded curtain, encrusted with gold and silver thread, cordons off the sleeping quarters. The more public area contains comfortable chairs and sofas. A beautifully carved table holds an exquisite chess set. The Count smiled as we entered and invited me to sit opposite him.

Father left us as we began to play. The board is of marble. The pieces are red and white gold, cool to the touch and incredibly heavy.

"I read of such a thing in a book of your British myths and legends," he told me. "I so liked the idea I had my own set made in Constantinople."

We play. Every night it is the same. I am nervous, because I'm not very good. He is far superior to me, but he lets me win – some of the time, anyway.

"Would you like tea?" he asks, after the third or fourth game.

Ivan, his manservant, appears as if from nowhere. Cook is right, he is huge; but so quiet and still, he can be in the room the whole time and you would never notice. He wears the clothes of his country, peasant dress, a loose, coarse-woven woollen tunic, and wide leather belt, over black breeches and knee-length boots. He makes tea in a samovar and we drink it like the Russians from little glasses with no milk. The Count shows me how to suck it through cubed sugar. He offers me tiny cakes, iced and delicious, but takes none himself.

As I eat, he tells me of his home. A land beyond the forests; far, far to the east, at the meeting point of Europe and Asia. And of his castle there, up in the mountains, set on a pinnacle. So high the eagles nest below it, and the mighty river, running at the bottom of the ravine, looks like a thin strip of steel. He talks on and on. I sip my tea and listen. It sounds a wild place, romantic and wonderful...

The first time, Father came to collect me. Other times Ivan accompanies me back to my own quarters. I'm always surprised when it is time to leave. Hours seem to have fled by like so many minutes.

"Again, I have kept you too long. I am so sorry."

He takes my fingers and kisses them. Again, I feel a slight sting on my palm. He turns my hand and kisses it just above the wrist. It is still a queer sensation, but I no longer find it unpleasant.

I have noticed that, when he smiles, he rarely shows his teeth. I find myself glad of it. They are by far his worst feature. If they were otherwise, his looks would be almost perfect. They are not irregular, but they are unusual. The front ones are small, slightly backward sloping, sharp-edged, with tiny serrations. The canines, either side, are large and an odd shape, pointed, almost conical. They are pearly, semi-translucent, more the colour of bone than teeth. No, that analogy is not correct. I have to think *about this. The thing they most resemble is the quill of a feather. I glimpsed them tonight, before his full lips shut them off from view. They are like those of another type of creature, something which belongs to a different species altogether. I try not to look at them, but feel compelled to do so. They give me an odd feeling inside as if something were not quite right—*

"Ellen. ELLEN! Supper's ready. Are you deaf, child? I've been calling and calling you!"

"Sorry, Gran," she shouted back. "Had my Walkman on. Be there now."

Ellen reluctantly put the diary back under the bed and walked slowly to the door, the words that she had just read resonating in her head. The teeth. The crypt. The castle. The land beyond the forests – that was Transylvania. Ellen didn't want any supper – she just wanted to know what was going to happen next. You didn't need to be a genius to work it out. It was harder to tell about the cousin, she didn't fit the profile quite so well, but there could be no doubt about the Count, it had been clear from Diary Day 1: he was definitely a vampire!

5

The drawing room was studded with the family past. Silver frames covered most available surfaces and one wall was a mass of photographs. Ellen's own generation were ranked along the sideboard and on the piano. Colour marked them out from the others and, apart from the school ones, they were less consciously posed, more informal. Most of them had been there for as long as she could remember. Ellen did not even know who most of them were. The only notice she had ever taken was to rearrange them now and again, to give herself and Karen prominence over various cousins. She had dismissed the others as photos of old people, and therefore of no interest; but now, on closer inspection, she realized it was only the cracking black and white and faded sepia that made them seem that way – the people within the pictures were not old at all.

"That was my brother, Anthony," her grandmother said.

She pointed to a fair-haired young man, who looked

about twenty, twenty-one, standing with a gang of others. They were squinting into a powerful sun, and laughing as if one of them had just cracked a joke. They were all dressed the same, in khaki shorts and short-sleeved shirts, and were draped on or about an enormous tank.

"He was killed in the Western Desert. And that is your great-great-uncle Thomas." She indicated another soldier, handsome and confident, formally posed in the uniform of the previous war. "Killed at Ypres. And there's me. I was in the WRENS. That's how I met Grandad. I was his driver."

Ellen studied the young woman, fair hair rolled up under a peak cap, large eyes gazing steadily out from under high arched, finely shaped brows. She was not smiling but her full lips and wide mouth were emphasized by the dark lipstick of the time and the photograph's black and white. The fitted uniform jacket, pencil skirt and black stockings, flattered her long legs and slender figure.

"You were very attractive."

Her grandmother laughed. "There is no need to sound so surprised!"

"I was wondering," Ellen started, "are there any of Ellen Laidlaw-Macmillan, my great-great-grandmother?"

"Let me see..." Her grandmother frowned and adjusted her glasses. "There should be at least one... Up there, on the left." She pointed with a forefinger permanently bent to the right with arthritis. "That's what she looked like when I knew her."

The person she was pointing at was not smiling either. In fact, she looked kind of frightening. Her hair was scraped into a tight bun and she frowned down, head held high, her eyes distant. Her dress, buttoned up to the neck, was of dark shiny silk stuff. One of those upside-down watches nurses wear was pinned to a formidable bosom.

"I didn't mean then. I meant when she was younger."

Her grandmother scanned the wall from end to end, in vain.

"I thought there were. There used to be. I remember seeing pictures of her as quite a young girl." She shrugged. "Goodness knows where they are now. This house eats things, I'd swear to it." She put her hand on Ellen's arm. "Come and sit down. I got some of those little almond biscuits you like and your drink will be getting cold."

Ellen suppressed a shudder. Her gran was a great believer in milky drinks – that was one of the only drawbacks about coming to stay with her.

"Do you remember her?" she asked, putting the large mug she had been passed down by the side of her chair.

"Extremely well! Although I was still quite young when she died – a little older than you, I suppose, and children don't take much notice of old fogeys." She paused, considering. "She was always rather grand, rather distant. We'd be wheeled along at birthdays, Christmas, to take tea with her, that kind of thing. In this very room." She looked round at the pleasant, comfortable furniture, the Laura Ashley wallpaper, and smiled. "It was not quite as it is now. A maid ushered us in and out and we had to be on our very best behaviour. She was always frightfully busy, I do remember that. What with the practice, hospital work and her research – she worked almost up to the day she died. Exceptional woman for her time, for any time, quite extraordinary. Of course, in those days, it was a fearful struggle for a woman even to qualify as a doctor, let alone gain recognition and make a name for herself, in the way she did."

"What about her husband?"

"I saw less of him than her. He was always out visiting patients. He was very tall, with twinkly eyes, and used to give us peppermints out of his waistcoat pocket. He died before her, as I recall. They were very close. Mother said she used her work as an escape, a substitute."

"You don't know anything about when she was young?"

"I'm afraid I don't. Why the sudden interest?"

"We did a project – at school – about women achievers. I just wondered what she was like, you know, as a person."

"Mother donated her books and papers to a medical research institute. You might find something in the library. They've got a collection of people recalling the past. She was quite a well-known local personality. If it's a nice day tomorrow, you could ask Andrew to take you."

"That's if I ever see him again," Ellen said, almost to herself.

"Oh, my dear –" her grandmother clapped her hand to her mouth – "he telephoned earlier, while you were resting. It totally went out of my mind. I *am* getting forgetful. I'm awfully sorry. He said tomorrow was his free afternoon and he'd be round about lunchtime. I said as long as you felt strong enough. Is that all right?"

"Yes, that's fine."

She felt strong enough. She felt perfectly well. Ellen sat back, sipping her Horlicks. She had not had any for years and it didn't taste too bad after all.

Ellen had meant to go back to the diaries, and her great-great-grandmother's story, as soon as she regained her own room, but the milk drink made her sleepy and she found it hard to focus on the small neat writing. Her mind began to stray from the far distant past to the immediate future. What would the weather be like tomorrow? Would she be able to think of things to say? And would she be OK? She had not been out of the house for days. Would she be able to stand the pace, without fainting or anything embarrassing like that happening to her?

The book became heavy, slipping from her hands. She could no longer fight it, her eyes were beginning to close. Only one thought trespassed as she reached to turn off the light. Vampires exist in stories, in late-night horror movies. But this diary contained the true writing of an actual person. This diary was real.

6

When she woke in the morning, sunlight lay in a solid bar across the bed. Ellen drew her curtains. It looked cold but the sky was blue and cloudless. She checked herself for signs of weakness and found none. She was feeling better than she had for weeks, and optimistic. For the first time for ages she was looking forward to something. The mirror confirmed how good she felt. The face looking back was no longer so watered down and washed out. After a shower, she added more colour to her cheeks and hid what remained of the rings under her eyes with make-up.

Andrew arrived at five to twelve. Her grandmother insisted on scarf and gloves and made sure she buttoned her coat up but, other than that, they left the house with the minimum of fuss.

Outside, it was cold enough for their breath to show. Frost lingered along the sides of walls like lines of white shadow, but the sun still retained a little warmth and the air smelt good enough despite the traffic.

Andy took her hand to cross the road and did not let go.

He linked arms as they wandered along the High Street, looking in windows, visiting one shop, then another. Ellen need not have worried about having nothing to say. They talked non-stop, about anything and everything. More than that, he made her laugh. Something no one else had been able to achieve for quite a time.

One of the side streets was occupied by a market. It was a pretty ramshackle collection, but Ellen noticed a couple of junk stalls dotted here and there among the cheap clothes, sports label rip-offs, plastic tack and dodgy electrical equipment. The goods arrayed for inspection made the average car boot sale look like Sotheby's, but among other newly discovered common interests, they shared a taste for old things, potential bargains.

"You never know what you might find," they said together, and laughed.

Andy was always on the lookout for old LPs and plastic toys for his kitsch collection. He started sorting through the bootleg CDs and cardboard boxes of albums while Ellen drifted over to the piles of old books. Most of them looked distinctly unpromising, rows of dog-eared paperbacks and a jumble of musty-smelling hardbacks, library throw-outs with cracked spines and blotting-paper pages. She was just about to turn away when a title caught her eye.

WOMEN IN MEDICINE

Following on from her conversation with her grandmother the night before, she flipped to the back of the book, to check the index, and there she was:

Laidlaw-Macmillan, Dr Ellen Isobel, 60–61

Ellen turned to the pages indicated:

Dr Ellen Laidlaw-Macmillan (1862–1938) was also a student at the London School of Medicine for Women in the 1880s. She was to prove a major figure in the modern study of the blood. Her publication of the papers of her father (Dr Anthony Laidlaw), and her own research work based on his findings, are widely acknowledged as having made a considerable contribution to the discovery of human blood groups. This, in turn, made safe transfusion possible and has, without doubt, saved many millions of lives. Laidlaw-Macmillan is particularly regarded for her work on the so-called "Blue Baby Syndrome" caused by antibody reaction to rhesus negative blood types. This had been a major cause of perinatal death and, again, her discoveries contributed to the saving of many lives.

"Interesting?" Andy asked as he came over, a couple of LPs tucked under his arm.

"Yeah, kind of."

"Buy it," he said, looking over her shoulder, "it's only 50p. Here you are, mate." He handed the stallholder a coin. "Come on," he turned to Ellen, "I'm starving. I know this great place just round the corner from here – they do lunchtime specials. As much pasta as you can eat. It's only £3.50."

Ellen was not all that hungry, but Andy more than made up for her. He went back for third and fourth helpings. You could have unlimited coffee afterwards: he took advantage of that offer as well.

"Is that what you want to be?" He indicated the book on the table next to Ellen. "A doctor?"

"No, not really." She shook her head.

"What do you want to do? In the future?"

Ellen shrugged. "I don't know. I don't think about it."

She grew silent. Closed off. This was not a favourite topic. Over the last year, since her condition had developed, everything had become uncertain. She had learnt not to plan, not even to think about the future. No one could say for certain whether she had one.

"It's a good career. If you like sciences," Andy went on, trying to get her to respond. "Do you?"

"Do I what?"

"Like sciences."

She did, actually. Maths came easily. She liked logic and order and was naturally curious. Or had been, until all her energy had been taken away by this bewildering disorder.

"They're OK," she replied, noncommittally.

He made a face. "I don't."

"What do you want to do, then?"

He laughed. "When I grow up? Who says I'm going to? Seriously, I want to go into computer graphics. I'm doing, like, art and design at the moment, and then I intend to…"

She listened as he outlined his plans. He had it all worked out. Colleges. Courses. Job opportunities. It must be nice to see your whole life stretching out in front of you. It must be nice to feel that way.

"What's the matter?" he asked suddenly.

"Nothing." She looked up into his blue eyes. "Why?"

"It's just –" he took her hand – "it's just, for a moment, you looked really, I don't know, sad or something."

"No. I'm fine."

"So?" He pointed to the book again. "Why the interest?"

"Oh," Ellen smiled now, "it's got a reference to my great-great-grandmother in it. She was kind of famous. I was talking to Gran about her last night." She paused, wondering whether to tell him or not. "I found her diaries, up in the attic. They were in that box, the one you brought down for me the other day."

"Interesting? Or full of boring doctor stuff…"

"Not at all! She kept them when she was young, the ones I'm reading anyway. They're fascinating – kind of weird—"

"Weird? In what way?" Something about her face, the look in her eyes, alerted his interest.

"This is going to sound strange, really odd, but it seems, it seems like – I don't quite know how to put this…"

Ellen frowned, suddenly unsure. Sometimes she found it difficult to believe what she'd read herself. She didn't really know him that well; if she told him what she suspected, he might think she was some kind of nutcase.

"What? Seems like what?"

"Well, from reading it – in the diaries – it seems as if my great-great-grandmother was involved with a vampire."

She said it quickly and sat back, watching him, trying to gauge his reaction.

"Really!" He wasn't staring at her in disbelief. He wasn't laughing as though she was crazy. "Well? Go on! Don't keep me in suspense. Tell me about it!"

He leaned forward, captivated, as she repeated Ellen's story. He let his coffee go cold and listened with complete seriousness as she went on to explain her theory about the true nature of the Count Szekelys and his sinister cousin.

"Can I read them?" he asked, when she had finished.

"Of course!"

"I could pick them up when we go back."

She shook her head. "I haven't read it all myself yet."

"Tomorrow?"

"Sure – if you're interested."

"Oh, I'm interested."

"That's a relief." Ellen grinned. "I was in two minds about whether to tell you, in case you thought I was some kind of loony."

"I wouldn't think that…"

It was time to go. Andy reached in his pocket to pay the bill.

"I'll get it," Ellen said.

"Hey, no…"

"Gran gave me money. And Mum left me lots. I don't usually get a chance to spend it."

She took out her wallet, and found a couple of notes.

"Oh, all right," he agreed reluctantly, "if you insist…"

"I do, absolutely," she replied, handing the money to the waiter.

"This time I'll let you, but next time…"

So there was going to be a next time. Ellen used the cover of accepting her change to hide a secret smile.

Andy didn't notice. He stood up and helped her with her coat, his mind still on the diaries. He had his own reasons for believing in vampires.

When they got outside, the brightness of the day had gone. The sun had already disappeared behind a high ridge of tall houses. Without its warmth the air bit with the promise of a frosty night. A ghostly crescent moon, thin as a nail paring, already lay in wait behind the branches of trees stripped of their last leaves.

"I promised your gran I wouldn't keep you out too

long." Andy guided her towards a pair of tall wrought-iron gates. "We'll go through the cemetery. It's quicker."

A broad asphalt path, flanked by carefully tended flower beds, provided a public way from one side to the other. Near it, the plots were neat, small and fairly uniform, the grass between them kept short. Floral tributes and wreaths lay on the graves of those still remembered by the living. New additions were signified by raw patches of earth and flimsy wooden crosses, bunches of flowers rotting away inside soggy cellophane wrapping.

Further from the path there were no signs of recent remembrance. Nature had taken over. The oldest part of the cemetery contained monuments from a different age, one that did not seek to hide death but used it to display wealth and importance. Polished granite columns soared, and carved figures presided over extravagant tombs. Victorian mausoleums, green with algae, grey with London grime, stood above ground, large as houses, providing the resting place for whole families. The Council and the Preservation Society were gradually cutting the wilderness back, instituting restoration, but funds were short and many areas remained overgrown, out of bounds to the general public.

Near the middle was a small stone chapel. Outside it there was a blackboard advertising the time of the next guided tour.

"Lots of famous people are buried here," Andrew commented as they walked past. "But it's kind of a job to find them. That's why they have the tours."

"Do you remember that time when you came in here for a dare and came out all white-faced and trembly?"

"I wasn't!"

"Yes, you were! You went straight home. Karen and I watched you walk past the house from the front bedroom. I was desperate to know what happened, but when you came round the next day you wouldn't talk about it."

"Well, I do remember, as it happens. It must have been somewhere over there…"

Andrew cleared his throat and then laughed; the memory of his former fear suddenly made him nervous. He swept his hair out of his eyes to squint into the distance to where marble gleamed in the darkening thickets.

"First of all, I kind of got a bit lost." He laughed again. "The guided tours are probably a good idea. Anyway, I was just finding my way back, when one of the Preservation blokes spotted me. He started shouting and he was waving this big stick. So I dodged round the side of one of those big marble jobs. It had a kind of door, but it had been all bashed in by vandals, so I had a look. It had a paved passage, like a regular house. I went in…"

"Weren't you frightened?"

He shook his head. "Not then. More curious. I just wanted to see what was inside. I even remember being a bit disappointed because there weren't even any coffins, let alone bodies. Just, like I said, this passageway with like bricked-up doors leading off it…"

"And?"

"And, well, that's when I heard it." Despite himself, he shivered at the memory. "It was coming from behind the furthest doorway, a kind of scratching…"

"It was probably rats…"

"Or foxes – there's lots of urban foxes in here – that's what I thought. But, well, it *sounded*, it sounded like fingernails scraping on stone. Long ones. And I remembered reading somewhere that nails carry on growing after a person is dead and it was kind of slow, deliberate, not like an animal…"

Ellen shuddered. "No wonder you were scared. I'd have legged it straight out of there."

"That was the weird thing." He looked down at her, his blue eyes clouded and troubled. "I couldn't. Everything in me was screaming 'Run! Run!' but I couldn't break away, I just kept going towards it, one step and then another, until…"

"Until what?"

"There was shouting outside. The old guy with a stick must've seen me dodge in. He was banging on what was left of the door and yelling for me to come out. The scratching stopped. And – this was odd – I could feel it kind of withdrawing, like it was releasing me, but reluctantly. I was out of there in seconds flat, steaming past the old bloke – he went flying. He started after me, stick going, but they aren't very fast on their pins, and I was running like the wind. I didn't slow down until I was out of the gates. I made myself stop then, I had to get my breath back to come past your house. I still don't know how I made it home, my legs were shaking that bad."

"That's *really* scary." Ellen regarded him seriously. "That is one of the scariest things anyone has ever told me."

"Yeah, but that's not the worst of it. A couple of years ago, I was doing this local history thing for school and I came across this article about vampires."

"What? Here! You're kidding me!"

"No. Really. A whole nest of them, apparently. Right

here. In this cemetery. And I'm not talking olden days, I'm talking this century. There have been all sorts of rumours. Stories about sightings in the graveyard, and outside."

"Where outside?"

"By the gates. Opposite where your gran lives. Some sort of ghostly figure suddenly appears, late at night, scaring the life out of people. It has happened so many times it has to be more than coincidence. There have been vampire hunters. Serious investigations. I've got a bunch of cuttings at home. I'll show you if you like, if you are interested."

It was Ellen's turn to shiver. Darkness had been falling even as they had been talking, and a thin mist was sliding out of the trees and creeping along the sides of the graves towards them.

"We'd better get going." Andy put his arm round her. "They lock the gate soon after sundown."

They had just set off, when Ellen suddenly stopped. She sensed rather than saw a flicker of movement far to the right. Something black, a shadow in the thickening mist, flitting between the tombstones. It moved when they moved, stopped when they stopped. She had a sudden powerful sensation of being watched. Whatever, whoever it was, seemed to mirror their movements exactly.

"What's the matter?"

"I thought I saw something."

"Where?"

"Over there. In the trees. Somebody moving parallel, following…"

"I can't see anything…" Andy squinted down her line of sight.

"He's gone now."

Ellen hunched her shoulders as they started for home. It must have been a trick of the light. The figure had melted out of sight. Still, she would not like to be caught in here much after sundown.

Andy walked her back but refused her invitation to come in.

"I've got some work to do," he said with a shake of the head. "You'd better get in or your gran'll be cross with me and won't let me see you again."

He leaned towards her, intending to give her a goodbye kiss on the cheek, but just at that moment Ellen turned her head and he found her mouth instead. His lips were warm on hers, contrasting with the cool surface of his skin. He put his arms round her. She was so slight, lost inside her big coat, as if there was almost nothing there, just air. He held her close, wanting to protect her, save her, always be there for her.

"Ellen? Is that you?"

They broke away from each other as the porch light went on and footsteps sounded in the hall.

"Yes, Gran…"

"Don't stand about in the cold. You'll catch a chill."

The front door was already opening as Andy blew her a kiss and moved away towards the street. He waved as he reached the pavement.

" 'Bye, Ellen," he called. "Be seeing you."

7

Ellen had tried to hide it from Andy, she so wanted him to see her and treat her like an ordinary girl, somebody normal, but she was worn out, exhausted. Once inside, she did not know how long she could carry on, but if she was going to be allowed to see him again, she had to disguise it. It was lucky Gran went to bed early, she was not going to last much longer.

"'Night, dear," her grandmother called from the landing.

"'Night, Gran," Ellen called back. "Thanks for the Horlicks."

The milky drink formed skin as she lay back on the bed. One of the worst states to be in. Bone tired but not at all sleepy.

There was one thing she could do to while away the time. She reached under the bed for the other Ellen's diary.

10th February, 1878

This evening I was summoned to Papa's laboratory. Tom and Papa were arguing so furiously they did not even notice my entrance. Papa was collecting pieces of apparatus, stands, bottles, rubber tubing. Tom was following him around, protesting.

"Dr Laidlaw! Listen to me! I think this course of action most ill advised." He caught hold of Father's arm. "It is dangerous in the extreme, not to say illegal! If you insist on carrying it out he may well die!"

Father turned to him. "If I do not he will die anyway. He is dying now. You have seen him. Tell me, Tom — you have tended the dying — is not death upon him? If not tonight, he will go tomorrow. Even an untrained eye could see it."

Tom released my father's arm and looked down with a slight nod of the head.

"Now. Are you willing to assist me, or not?"

Again, the slight nod of the head.

"Well, then. Assist me by carrying this. The sooner we get this over, the quicker he will recover."

At this point they turned to see me standing just inside the door.

"Ah, Ellen," Papa greeted me, "I would like you to come with us to attend the Count. His condition has deteriorated and…"

"Dr Laidlaw!" Tom started again. "A girl should not witness, have to attend…"

"Nonsense!" Father cut him off. "Are there no nurses in the London Hospital?"

"Yes, but Ellen is a young lady!"

Father turned on him, even sterner than before.

"A young lady who wishes to be a doctor! She is no stranger to the sick bed. She has accompanied me on ward rounds, and on visits, and shown more intelligence, courage, and plain common-sense, than most young fool medical students I've had to deal with!"

"I'm sorry, I only meant…"

"Besides," Papa interrupted him, "the Count has taken a liking to her. He may derive comfort from her presence."

On our way to the Count's quarters, Father tried to warn me, but nothing could have prepared for the shock when I saw him. He was lying on a raised dais, almost like a bier. His arms on the counterpane were so wasted they looked like lengths of corded rope. His face was whiter than the sheets. No, that is wrong. It was of an entirely different colour. He looked as though his features had been carved from the palest ivory. He lay motionless, like a funereal figure. Only the slightest movement of the eyeballs under the lids persuaded me that we were not already too late.

Tom set up the necessary apparatus, while my father explained to me what they were going to do.

"We intend to give this young man a transfusion. That is to transfer, by means of this tubing, blood from one of us to him. Now, as I'm sure you heard Tom say, this is a highly dangerous procedure. Not to the donor, who suffers only a minor discomfort followed by perhaps a little tiredness, but to the recipient, who may die. For this reason it is illegal. But it is his only hope of life. Now you have seen him, Ellen. What do you say?"

"About what, Papa? Surely you don't need my permission?"

His dark eyes remained on me, searching, probing. The full enormity of what he proposed dawned slowly. The blood he intended to use would be my own!

Tom realized at about the same time as I did. His face became rigid.

"Dr Laidlaw. Sir," he said stiffly, "may I have a word with you?"

He pulled himself up to his full height and almost dragged my father away from the Count's bedside. Their conversation was carried on in a far corner, in fierce whispers, but I caught most of it.

"She is your own daughter!"

"She will suffer no harm, I assure you."

"But, I fail to understand how you can…" He left the words unsaid, his voice expressed all the shuddering horror I myself felt at the prospect. "Why don't you do it!"

"My blood is tainted. I suffer from a recurring infection. Do I have to explain further?"

"Use mine then!"

"No. You are entirely unsuitable. Look at you, and then look at him. You are different, in height, build, eye colour, hair colour, everything. We do not know, yet, what allows one blood to mix with another, but I think race could well be a factor. Your blood would curdle in his veins and kill him within minutes."

"How do you know hers will not?"

"I know. That is all. Now, we are wasting time…" He made to break away but Tom would not release him. "Very well, I will tell you. This has happened before." He indicated the lifeless form on the bed. "My own blood, as well as that of Isobel, Ellen's mother, both our bloods were used to transfuse. I cannot say for certain, but I am 99 per cent sure Ellen's blood will mix with his and not curdle." He sighed impatiently. "Would you let a man die because of your sensibilities? Ellen," he gestured in my direction, "is willing, if it will save him. Aren't you, child?"

I nodded, swallowing hard. To refuse was to watch a man die. What choice did I have? My father turned back to Tom, his face twisted with sneering contempt.

"She is showing herself to be more of a doctor now than you will ever be!"

With that, my father wrenched his arm away and returned to my side. I slowly folded back my sleeve while he prepared a swab, dousing gauze in antiseptic. Pride that Father was putting so much trust in me did little to counter the sick feeling in my stomach. Then Ivan, the Count's manservant, rose from the shadows at the end of the bed. The sleeve of his tunic was already rolled to expose an arm the colour and thickness of a beam of polished oak.

"Young doctor is right," his deep voice creaked and grated. He formed the words slowly, as though he was not used to speaking at all, let alone in English. "You will not use her. It is not..." he searched for the word, "...correct. You will use me. We are," he looked down at his master, "same volk. Same..." he paused again to translate, "...same race, same family."

Father opened his mouth to protest. He was not used to interference, particularly from minions, but his voice was cut off. Fingers, broad, long, and iron strong, closed round his neck. Ivan picked my father up as if he weighed no more than a child and shook him like a dog.

"You will use me. Understand?"

Father could not speak. He could scarcely even move his head to indicate his assent.

From then on the whole operation was conducted in silence.

The tubing was attached and Ivan sat, motionless and impassive, as pint after pint drained out of him into his master. My father went back and forth, muttering to himself, adjusting the apparatus. Tom stood by, clearly agitated, thinking Father had taken leave of his senses. He has not seen him like this. I have. I have known him shut himself away in his laboratory for days, weeks at a time, scarcely stopping to eat, let alone sleep. Hunting down disease to its source, searching endlessly for a cure. The Count and his mystery illness has started him off again, reawakened his obsession.

He stopped pacing and stared down at his patient. He had used all his powers as a doctor, now he exerted pure will to complete the treatment. The effect on the Count was truly miraculous. His limbs, so emaciated and thin, seemed to become plump and rounded. Even his hair seemed to thicken and take on a deep red lustre. His colour changed from ghastly ivory to parchment white. Then a pink blush crept across his countenance and he began to stir. At last he opened his eyes. He looked round us all, as though puzzled as to why we should be there to see him wake, and then he smiled.

"Ellen!" His gaze fixed on me. "I was dreaming about you. Now here you are!"

11th February, 1878

Father tells me that the Count is responding well. He

slept peacefully and seems on the way to a full recovery. Ivan was in the kitchen this morning. He waited, silent as ever, while Cook just ignored him. She had instructions to fry liver for him, but was taking her time about it. Marie wrinkled her nose and said something I couldn't catch but it sounded contemptuous. They both glanced at him, laughing. I told them, quite sharp, that they had no right to question my father's orders and that Ivan was a guest and as such would be treated with respect. Cook prepared his breakfast at the expense of my own, but I do not care. It seems to me that, as a stranger, Ivan should be treated with kindness, not suspicion.

He thanked me with a slight incline of the head, and with his eyes. They are dark brown, quick and intelligent, set deep in folds of skin permanently creased against wind and weather. He might not speak but he misses nothing. I sense that he lives by an ancient and simple code. My willingness to give my blood last night seems to have earned me his respect and now, by extending my protection, I have gained his gratitude and, I think, his loyalty.

13th February, 1878

The Countess was there when I returned from school. She had been visiting her kinsman. I still do not like her. Her gratitude to my father is extravagant and unnecessary. I want to say to her: "He is a doctor. It is his job." But I said nothing, just put up with her simpering and gushing. Perhaps it is because she is foreign, or because I am not used to physical demonstrations of affection, but I do not like the way she paws and pets me. I find her touch repulsive and it grows harder to hide my irritation.

57

14th February, 1878

*Tonight I am to visit the Count but I walked home with
Tom uppermost in my mind. I fear a rift between him
and my father and I wanted to see him, to talk to him, but
it appears he is still too busy with his other concerns to
bother with me.*

*I arrived at the house to find Cook, Mrs Dover, and
Marie all standing outside the side entrance. I joined
them, curious to see what had called them from their
duties, just in time to witness a dismal little procession
coming up from the river. Two police constables were
carrying a makeshift stretcher made from half a door. A
roughly lashed piece of tarpaulin covered their small
burden. Behind them came a woman and a ragged line of
children. The woman was sobbing, a shawl, patched and
darned and then patched again, covered her face. The
children's faces, darkened with grime, were impassive.
Their feet were bare, despite the cold, and their clothes
little more than a collection of rags tied up with rope.*

They did not even glance in our direction as they filed past.

*"Young lad been missing a couple of days. They just
found him dead in the river," Cook told me, by way of
explanation. "Mudlark most like." By this I took her to
mean he is one of the boys that haunt the shoreline,
scavenging for what they can find. "Must've fallen in and
got took by the current, then got caught up in propellers,
or somethin'. One of the lightermen fished him out. All
slashed about the neck and chest, he was, terrible bad."*

"How do you know?" I asked, as we went inside.

*It was a silly question. Cook knows everything. Her
vast family extends through the whole of the East End and*

a constant stream of tradesmen visit the kitchen. She is always willing to offer tea, and whatever has just come warm from the oven, for the latest gossip or some tasty scrap of information.

"Donald, our Renee's eldest, was down on the wharf when they brung him in. How's yer 'and?"

"Fine, thanks."

"That little cut still troubling?"

"Not any more."

"Take off yer glove. Let's have a look."

She took my right hand in her thick red fingers and turned it over. I have suffered a small injury, just above the wrist; it caught on my clothes and would not heal. It was not painful, and did not bleed, but it kept opening up like a ragged little mouth. Ever since Cook spotted it, she has insisted on applying a poultice. She spent part of her childhood living with her grandma in Suffolk and, although she calls herself a Cockney and affects to despise the country, she has planted a small cottage garden within our high walls and grows her own herbs and vegetables. Mrs Dover calls her "cures" mumbo jumbo, and warned against "The Doctor" (meaning my father) "finding out". But he wouldn't mind. He shows a lot of interest in Cook's country remedies. This particular one consists of mouldy bread and leaves of wild garlic, which grows in part of the grounds, pounded together into a paste and then applied and kept on by a bandage. When she unwrapped it, the wound had gone, healed completely.

"There you are, see!" Cook exclaimed triumphantly. "You can keep your new-fangled medicines, can't beat the old-fashioned remedies."

15th February, 1878

Last night I was too tired to write. Time seems to melt when I am with the Count. His subterranean apartment with its candlelight and rich brocades and furnishings seems not to belong to any time or place, it is more like something out of a fairy-tale. Just like a visitor to a fairy realm, however much I try, I always lose track of the hours. I never realize, until I return to my own rooms, how very late it is. Sometimes I think the Count has more than earthly powers. I am letting my imagination run away with me. I blush to think what Papa would think if he read such foolish romantic nonsense. "Stick to the facts, Ellen," is what he says. "Stick to the facts."

The Count is much recovered. In fact, he was looking better than he has all the time I have known him. He was at his most entertaining. This time, with the small sugar cakes, he offered me wine. He poured it from a small glazed earthenware bottle into a tiny glass of cut crystal. The golden wine is intensely sweet, full of meadow flowers and summer heat. He watched me drink. Maybe it was the flickering candles but his eyes seemed a different colour tonight: tawny yellow with spikes of grey, like splinters of frost, surrounding the pupils.

"You like it?" he asked. "It is wine of my country. Very old, very rare. The secret of its making lost in time. Do not drink too fast. It is very strong. A little lasts long."

I sipped the wine slowly and listened as he told me stories of his strange land, of knights and princes, secret brotherhoods, desperate battles and heroic actions. It seems that his country is at the very gateway of Europe. His ancestors, and the people they commanded, were all that stood between the unprotected plains and the Turkish hordes. All there was to stop them sweeping down and laying waste to towns and cities, destroying everything in their path, putting all opposition to the sword, laying waste to civilization and Christianity.

Time and again they were beaten back, at terrible cost, until at last they came no more. My knowledge of history is small but it seems to me that this must have happened centuries ago, and yet it is as if he was there, so vivid is the detail, as if he was recounting a memory still fresh in his head.

His most affecting tale was of a young prince, captured and held by the Turks for ransom. He was kept as an honoured guest and learnt much from his captors about magic, alchemy and occult practices, but when he returned to his native land he found he had been betrayed. His castle was in ruins, all the inhabitants put to the slaughter, including his wife, his son and his little daughter. He lived amid the destruction, waiting for death to claim him, but it did not. So he rode out to seek it in the heat and smoking reek of battle, but still death would not take him. He was the one who drove the Turks from the doors of Europe. He possessed *extraordinary* daring, matched by extreme savagery and ruthless cunning. In his own country his name was spoken only in whispers and it meant "Dragon", "Eater of Men".

I sat spellbound while he told me this story. I know I will dream of it. I could see the wonders of the Caliph's court, hear the mutter of the viziers as they passed on their arcane knowledge. I heard his cry of anguish, echoing from mountain to mountain, and the curse he put on himself and God. I saw the tumult of battle, my ears seemed filled with the screams of dying men and horses.

When it was time for me to leave, he took my hand, apologizing, as always, for keeping me so long. He turned to kiss the underside, as is his custom, and then flinched away. His whole expression changed. His nose wrinkled, his lips drew back and he uttered a sound of disgust that was scarcely human, a sibilant hiss, formed far back in his mouth. His fingers, with their long pointed nails, released my own as if they carried some sort of current, like electricity.

"What is that?" He spat the words out, his accent harsh and pronounced.

For a moment, I was at a loss. I had no idea what he was talking about. Then I followed his gaze. He was staring at the base of my wrist, at the place where the poultice had been.

"I had a small cut. Cook applied one of her cures. It is better now."

"Your father should attend you..."

"I did not like to bother him."

"Next time, do so. Do not put your faith in folk remedies, some of the herbs the old wives use are noxious in the extreme."

I shrugged. I did not care for his tone. It was cold, as though he was ordering me. The moment jarred and his charm suddenly seemed like a mask held in place to hide a quite different personality.

"Forgive me. I should not have spoken so," he added, recovering himself. The façade was back, smooth as glass, as he sensed my displeasure. "It is late, and perhaps I overestimate my strength..."

"No. Not at all. I should not have kept you. It is my

fault." I turned to go. "I'm rather tired myself…"

"We must not part on a note of quarrel."

He looked anxious, apologetic. I forced a smile and said he was forgiven.

"Very well! Very good! Soon, Dr Laidlaw tells me, you have a holiday, is this not so?"

"Yes," I agreed, wondering at the sudden change of direction. "A few days…"

"Good. Very good. I have a surprise!"

"What?"

He smiled, revealing the tips of his peculiar teeth.

"If I told you, it would not be a surprise. Until then, I must rest. I have to regain my health. Good-night. Ivan will see you back to your apartment."

He turned with a wave and went back through the arras. For the first time I was glad to leave, glad to see him retreat into his private chamber.

Ivan padded along next to me, like a great cat. He moves very quietly for such a big man. I assumed, when I first saw him, that he was some kind of serf, but I have revised my opinion since then. His loyalty to the Count is unquestioning, bound by lines of fealty that go back for centuries, but I sense that Ivan is his own man and the dependency is with the Count, rather than the other way round.

The volume ended there. It was too late to start another tonight. She would lend this one to Andy and start the next in the morning. The entry she had just read made the case even more convincingly. This Count was a vampire. Had to be. That stuff about the garlic just confirmed it. Andy would be sure to see it, just as she did. It was odd, though. All through the last page, Ellen had wanted to scream "Get out of there!" but there was no hint anywhere that this other Ellen even suspected him. But then, why would she? Bram Stoker's *Dracula* hadn't even been written. There was no horror industry, back in 1878, churning out books and films. And even if there had been, Ellen thought about herself, if this was happening to her, would she believe it? The whole point about vampires and werewolves, and things like that, was that they lived on the screen, on the page, they did not exist in real life. You could walk out of the cinema, rewind the video, shut the book and leave them behind. Or could you? She remembered what Andy had said about whole nests of them in the cemetery across the road. Now. Not a hundred years ago. Ellen shivered.

Then she sneezed. Before she could reach for a tissue, she sneezed again. This was real ink, not print. If they existed then, they could exist now. Maybe they did. Maybe they were all around. She sniffed and lay the book down. Twenty-past one. Time to put out the light. She lay in the dark, thinking about the diaries, puzzling over what it all meant. The idea that she might have caught a cold simply did not occur to her.

Ellen's sleep was shallow, her night disturbed. Once or twice she started awake, thinking she heard something outside the window. Whatever it was sounded big and soft like a giant moth bumping up against the glass. It must be leaves from a nearby tree slapping against the pane. That explanation reassured her, allowing sleep to return.

Memory plays tricks in the night, in the dark. We imagine things not how they are, but how we want them to be.

No branches extended this far up the side of the house. The nearest tree was a sycamore and it had lost its leaves early.

8

Ellen Forrest woke to a new thought. If the Count was after this other Ellen, why didn't he make his move? Why didn't he pounce? He seemed to be playing with her. Why the elaborate game of cat and mouse? Maybe he had something else in mind. Maybe she wasn't just an ordinary victim. Ellen remembered stories she'd read, movies she'd seen. Sometimes vampires did that: kept the special ones until last. Ellen thumbed the rainbow borders of the next diary. For a moment, she was tempted to skip forward, like in a novel, to find out, but she stopped herself. This was a real person's life and to do that would be to show a kind of disrespect and, anyway, if she did that she might miss something, lose the thread, lose track of the story.

To find out what happened, she would have to read on. She had plenty of time. She wasn't, in fact, feeling all that well and Gran insisted that she stay in bed.

20th February, 1878

Another child has disappeared.

The child lives in one of the nearby streets. Last evening she was sent out by her mother, on some trivial errand, and has not returned. I came back from school to find that the search, begun at first light, has gone on all day. Men are out in the hospital grounds now—

I was called from my writing by a shout and the sound of running. I looked out of the window to see one of our men. His size and rough appearance mark him as an attendant from the asylum wing. He was walking back towards the house, shirt-sleeved, his coat wrapped round something in his arms. I could see by his face what the bundle contained. The child was taken straight to my father's consulting room, but when I got downstairs the faces all around told me that this was a mere formality.

Father emerged with a shake of his head.

"From her injuries," he announced as if he felt the need to stay something, "it appears she was knocked down and then run over by the wheels of a carriage some time last night. Death would have been instantaneous," he added, as if it might be of comfort. "I do not believe she suffered. One of the porters has already gone to inform the constabulary and the parents. There is nothing more we can do, so I suggest you all get back to your duties."

He turned, without another word, and everyone began to disperse.

"How'd she get in the grounds?" Marie asked, putting her hand to her mouth.

Cook sniffed and dabbed her eyes with her pinafore.

"Run down and then thrown over the wall, she was, poor little duck. If they ever find the beggar what done it – hanging's too good for 'em."

67

Later:

Papa and I had supper together. Not in the dining room, with its long polished table and gleaming silver, but in the parlour as we used to when I was younger. It is smaller in there, and cosy, a good fire glows in the grate and books line the walls – Father uses it as his study. Cook prepared chicken stew with little herb dumplings, usually one of my favourites, but the events of earlier in the evening had robbed us both of our appetites.

"I see death all the time, but when it is a child –" Papa stared into the fire as if seeking a response to a question for which there is no answer. "I don't know a medical man who is not upset by it."

His look was so bleak, so desolate, I went over to his chair and put my arms round him. He took me on to his knee and, for a moment, I was a child again, feeling the stuff of his waistcoat against my cheek, inhaling the faint scent of cigars which clings to him and, behind that, the hospital smell of ether and carbolic. It was like before… I grasp to define the time before – the time before what? I realize that what I mean is before the Count and his cousin came, forcing Papa away from me, into the salon and the laboratory, exerting their peculiar chemistry on both of us.

"Goodness," he said with a smile, holding me away from him. "How you have grown! Too heavy for my old bones!"

I felt the soft silkiness of his beard on my cheek and he released me.

"The Count is much recovered," he said, leaning forward to poke the fire alight. "He feels strong enough to take some excursions. He has asked me to ask you if you would be willing to accompany him."

"Of course!" So this is the "surprise" the Count spoke of. "When?"

"Any day convenient to you. When does your holiday start?"

"Next week."

"Next week it is then!"

"I thought he could not go out in the daytime. I remember you telling me he has an aversion to light."

"That seems to have abated somewhat with his improving condition. I have advised him to wear spectacles of smoked glass to protect his eyes."

"Where are we to go? What are we to do? I know little of London, and he will expect…"

I must have looked so perplexed, Papa laughed.

"That is all taken care of. The Countess, Elizabetta, knows London as well as she does Vienna…"

"Oh. Is she coming?"

At the thought of her the whole project began to lose its appeal. I found it hard to keep the disappointment out of my voice.

"Oh, yes. It was her suggestion. And," he regarded me over steepled fingers, "I have been thinking for some time… You are growing into a woman, my dear, and you have no mama…"

"I have you…"

He smiled. "I am a mere man. What do I know of the womanly arts? No. You need the help and guidance of one of your own sex…"

"There's Mrs Dover."

His laugh rang out, deep and musical. "Admirable as she is in many ways, I hardly think Mrs Dover is the right person to fit a young lady for society!"

"But Papa! I don't want... Why do I need...?"

I was stumbling through words, trying to find a way to express the feelings inside me. I sensed, far from going back, there is more change on the way. And I do not want to change. Into what? Why should I? I do not want to be "made fit for society". What "society"? And certainly not by her. Our eyes locked. The dancing amusement faded from his to be replaced by another look. I have seen it before. It means all argument is futile. He is as kind and good a father as it is possible to have but, once he has made up his mind, he becomes implacable. Nevertheless, I was determined to have my say. I opened my mouth again but just as I was about to speak there was a knock on the door.

It was Tom.

"Excuse me, sir. There is a policeman to see you."

Father rose and left Tom and me alone.

"Are you all right?" Tom asked. "What's the matter?"

"Nothing!"

I regretted my answer as soon as it was out of my mouth. I was upset with Father, not Tom, but the sharpness of my reply stung and brought conversation to a halt. I have hardly seen Tom to talk to since the night of the transfusion. It is not all that long, but something seems to have changed between us. We behave like a couple of strangers, even unable to exchange pleasantries. Our uncomfortable silence went on beyond the point where either of us knew how to break it. Awkward and ill at ease, looking at anything else but each other, we sat listening to the conversation coming through the half-closed door.

"Sorry to disturb you, Doctor Laidlaw. The name's

Mullholland. Sergeant Mullholland. City Detective Office. It's about the little girl that was found in your grounds..."

"You are investigating? I assumed, from her injuries, that her death was an accident..."

"Made to look that way, Police Surgeon reckons. We are treating it as a suspicious death. Now, sir. Some of your report I don't understand. This here, for example, 'lividity' and 'something sanguineous'," the poor man practically had to spell the last word out, "what does it mean, exactly?"

"It means blood," my father answered, "or rather lack of it. With injuries like that there should have been more. I thought it odd, that's all."

"What could account for it?"

"That depends. It could have drained from her – either at the scene or the place where she lay..."

"We've failed to find much at either of those places." There was a pause. "I just wondered if there could be any other cause ... you see there have been other cases..."

"I'm afraid I cannot help you. I'm a medical man. I just report what I find. You are the detective. Now, if you'll excuse me..."

"Just a few more questions, Doctor, if you don't mind... I was wondering," he cleared his throat, "seeing as this little girl was found in your grounds and there have been other incidents, of a similar kind, fairly adjacent, and given the nature of your establishment..."

"You think it might be one of my patients?" Father sounded irritated. This kind of prejudice annoyed him. "The poor souls in my care are a danger only to themselves. Not to anyone else. The asylum wing is *perfectly secure. You can inspect it, if you like. I can assure you, Sergeant, that whoever is doing this, it is not one of my patients."*

"Even so…"

Someone shut the door and we heard no more.

"Mrs Dover tells me you have a holiday coming up," Tom said after a while. "I have a few days owed, I was wondering if you would like to spend some time with me? We could…"

I put my hand up to stop him going any further.

"I'd love to, Tom," I said, "but I can't. Papa wishes me to accompany the Count and his cousin…"

"I see…"

A muscle jumped in his cheek and the eager, hopeful light in his eyes died away. How many times have I hoped and wished to hear him say that to me? Now, when he does, I have to refuse. I couldn't find words to say what I felt so, again, conversation failed between us. Just then Marie came in. Tom used her entrance as an excuse to leave.

"What's up with him?" Marie asked as she poured my tea.

She listened as I explained.

"Men!" Marie exclaimed, with a shake of her head. "Never say nothing till it's too late. He's only got hisself to blame. Cat's away…"

I asked what she meant.

"Shouldn't neglect you, should he? He don't like you spending time with the Count. If you ask me, he's jealous!"

Ellen put down the book, her reading interrupted by

voices from downstairs. One of them was male. She thought it might be Andy, but when she got out on the landing it was a voice she did not recognize. Deep and oddly accented, the speaker seemed to be thanking her grandmother for something.

"Not at all," she heard Gran say. "Call in any time. And thank you again for your help."

By the time Ellen reached the turn of the stairs, the front door was closed; all she could see was a tall figure rendered into outline shadow by the frosted glass.

"Who was that?" she called down.

"A chap I met, down by the cemetery gate. It's so slippy out, I turned my ankle. Shopping went everywhere. I felt so silly…"

"Are you all right?" Ellen came down towards her.

"Perfectly, dear. Don't fuss. You're getting as bad as your mother. That chap helped me, carried my shopping back. We got chatting. He has come into some property in the area. Old family place, been rented out, got a bit dilapidated. He's thinking about restoring it and was asking about period detail – this house has all the original features, so I asked him in to have a look round…" Edith Baxter looked down at her ankle. "It is swelling a little bit. I'd better rest it, I think."

"Do you want a cup of tea? I'll put the shopping away and bring you one in."

"That would be nice, dear."

"I'll just get dressed."

"There's no need…"

"I want to." Ellen called back. "Andy's coming round later."

*   *   *

Andy found her resting on the bed again. Getting up and looking after Gran had taken it out of her.

"Hi! It's only me."

He was carrying a folder filled with paper.

"Is that your vampire stuff?" Ellen asked.

"Yeah."

"Let's have a look."

"Aren't you hot in here?" Andy gave her the file and took off his coat. "I'm boiling."

"Open the window, if you like. It's Gran, she feels the cold, keeps the thermostat permanently on 'pass out'."

Andy went to the bay and pushed the side sash up a crack. He looked down at the graveyard. It did not look so sinister today. The freezing weather had lent it a sugar-frosting prettiness. It positively sparkled, on the surface, at least. There was still something dark, though, deep in the heart of it.

"Where are the diaries?" he asked, turning round. After yesterday's discussion he was anxious to see them.

"Oh." Ellen didn't look up from her quick flick through the cuttings. "Down by the bed. The one on top is the one I've read."

Andy pulled the box out. He whistled as he flipped it open.

"There are certainly enough of them. Should keep you busy for a bit."

"I didn't mean that!" Andy shook his head and knelt down to examine the contents of the box. She'd take it the wrong way, whatever he said. There was no talking to girls sometimes.

"There's other stuff besides books in here."

"Yeah, I know. I haven't had time to sort through all of it."

Andy moved some of the books and took out a photograph encased in thick card.

"That must be her…"

The face he was looking at stared back. The long hair, darkened in the photograph to nearly black, fell down over one shoulder. Her expression was grave, her head held up and slightly back. Her mouth was unsmiling, firm and resolute, the cleft chin underneath hinting at stubbornness. Between the finely arched eyebrows there was the shadow of a frown. Large eyes, grey and clear, gazed out, issuing a challenge to whoever happened to be regarding her.

"Hey, Andy." She looked up from the cuttings and her eyes met his. "There could be a pattern to this. I mean, look at the dates. These reports and sightings seem to happen in cycles. And they all seem to come from one place, one part of the cemetery. This tall, dark figure, and these other ones… What's up? What's the matter?"

He was staring at her as though she was a stranger.

The slight furrowing of her brow added the final matching detail. Andy's hand, holding the picture, tightened its grip until the cardboard creased. He looked at Ellen, then at the photograph, and then back to Ellen again, just to make sure. It was uncanny. The smile left his face. His stomach began to tense. Although the room was cool enough now, sweat broke out again on his forehead.

"Does she look like me?" Ellen asked. Half in jest.

"She doesn't just look like you," he replied. "She *is* you, Ellen."

9

Andy promised to come back later that evening. He could see that going out was not an option. However much Ellen was pretending, it was clear how ill she was. So he promised to bring along some home entertainment.

He arrived about eight o'clock, armed with videos and a large carrier bag.

"I've got popcorn, two sorts. A couple of bottles of Coke and ice-cream for the interval. I didn't know what kind you liked, so I got one plain and one with nuts and bits. Is that all right?"

He looked so concerned, Ellen laughed out loud and he grinned back. Her laughter was so rare these days it sounded odd even to her own ears. It was such a relief to be with someone who wasn't always serious.

"What films did you get?"

"'Interview with a Vampire' and 'Dracula'. Kind of deep background."

Ellen's grandmother shuddered. "I don't know how you young people can watch such things." She stood up.

"I'll leave you to it. Give me the ice-cream. It had better go in the freezer before it melts everywhere. I'll say good-night. I have a couple of letters to write and then I'm going to bed."

"Night, Gran."

"Good-night, Mrs Baxter."

"Ellen isn't well, remember," she said, turning to Andy. "Don't keep her up too late."

"No, I won't. I promise. I've read the diary," he said to Ellen after her grandmother left the room.

"What do you think?"

"I'd like to see the next one – when you finish it. It seems unbelievable – but when you think about what it says in that…" He indicated the file of newspaper cuttings which lay on the table. "If you put the two together…"

"Exactly." Ellen leaned forward. There was something she wanted to discuss with him. "You don't think it could happen now, do you? I mean, I've been reading this stuff – and being this close to the cemetery – it's beginning to give me the creeps."

"The diaries – that all happened a long time ago –" Andy put his hand on her shoulder, trying to reassure her – "the modern sightings were all outside, at night. You aren't going to go wandering around there after dark, are you?"

"What if they can get in? There was a girl. Look…"

She opened the folder to a picture taken from the local gazette. The girl had long hair, parted in the middle, sixties style. She was sitting on a bed, eyes fixed on the camera, a crucifix held out in front of her.

The headline read: *Vampire Girl Tells Of Terror Ordeal*.

Ellen shivered. She'd read the story. She had read all of

them several times and now she wished she had never asked to see his collection of clippings. The diaries were one thing; even if they were true she was separated from the events by more than a century. The newspaper stories made it much more real. Closer to home – literally.

"Let's face it," she added, leafing through, "they don't exactly have far to go."

Andy shook his head. "They have to be invited in. Vampires can't cross a threshold unless they are invited."

"How do you know?"

"I read it somewhere. Or maybe I saw it, in one of these movies. I know it's scary, but you mustn't let your imagination get the upper hand. Are you sure you want to see these? If you feel nervous about it, we could watch something else."

"Like what? You've brought them now. We might as well take a look."

The films had lost their power to frighten her. They were so obviously fictional, obviously unreal, that Ellen even felt soothed by them. She leaned back against Andy and it seemed only natural for him to put his arm round her as they shared a bowl of popcorn, and then for her to rest her head against his chest to watch the movie. She could relax into him, feel his heart beating. His presence was comforting. She was glad she'd shared the diaries with him.

Ellen was nearly asleep as the first film ended and Andy announced the interval. He went to get the ice-cream and they shared a second bottle of Coke. Ellen spooned up pralines 'n' cream and settled back to watch the trailers. Suddenly something cold slid down the front of her shirt.

"Hey! What are you doing?"

"That's what you do with this kind of ice-cream. You put it down people's shirts, I've seen it on the adverts. Didn't you know?"

"Right!" Ellen loaded her scoop and turned on him.

"Ellen! No!"

Edith Baxter smiled to herself as she heard the whoops and shrieks coming from downstairs. It was so good to hear Ellen laugh again. Stella would probably not approve, but she knew in her heart it would do no harm. Whatever ailed the girl, it was wrong to keep her away from the normal world. She must be allowed the freedom to behave like any other teenager.

"It's late." Andy pressed the remote to rewind the video and gently shifted Ellen's sleeping weight from his arm. "Ellen?" He pushed away the strands of hair that had fallen across her face. "Wake up. I have to go."

She opened her eyes, bewildered for a moment, and looked up into his. He was close, so close his image was blurring. Then her mouth met his. The video rewound itself and clicked off. A TV programme started up and went unnoticed. Eventually it was Andy who broke away. He opened his eyes wide, like he was waking up, and smiled.

"Hey," he said, "I really have to go…"

He stood up and went to retrieve his videos.

"Whatever I've got, it's not catching, you know," Ellen said as she handed him his coat.

"It's not that. It's just, if your gran comes down and finds me still here, I'll be banned for life and never be able to see you again…"

"Do you want to?"

He put his arms round her and kissed her again, light and quick.

"What do you think? Now I really must go." He zipped up his jacket. "I've got to be up bright and early."

"When will I see you? Tomorrow?"

"Not tomorrow. I'm going on a trip. Won't be back till late. Day after?"

"Promise?"

The central heating must have gone off, Ellen was beginning to shiver.

"Good-night."

"Night, Andy."

She went to see him out. A leaf blew in over the threshold. "Unless invited in…" Ellen knew it was silly, but she trapped it with her foot and edged it back on to the top step before shutting the door.

Andy went down the path. Even as the door closed, he wanted to see her again, talk to her. He had never felt like this about a girl. It was like he was only half in the real world. He had caught something all right, and whatever it was could be terminal. He was thinking this, and smiling to himself, as he rounded the corner where the short drive met the road. He turned sharply right and walked straight into someone.

Andy felt the shock, and registered the impact, with a swift intake of breath.

"I didn't see you. Sorry."

"Don't apologize. It was entirely my fault. Are you OK?" A gloved hand steadied his arm. "You seem shaken."

The deep voice sounded American, laced with a trace of some other accent.

"No, I'm fine," Andy replied. "I just wasn't expecting…"

He must have just been standing there, in the shadow of the tall hedge. There had been no sound, no warning footsteps. Andy looked up but could see little of his face under the wide fedora.

"If you are sure…" Teeth showed white, shining in the street light. "I'll bid you good-night."

The man touched the brim of his hat and walked away. The pavement glistened, frost lay thick; it might even have been snowing a little bit. The man's heels rang loud in the silence of the empty street. When he reached the corner, he glanced back for a second, and then he was gone. Andy looked down. He could see no footsteps in the whiteness on the ground.

Like many older people, Edith Baxter was a light sleeper. She had no idea what it was, but something caused her to wake in the early hours of the morning. She groped for her glasses and sat up in bed, listening for any noise from inside the house.

She could hear nothing, but still she got out of bed and found her robe. There was still no sound, just the distant ticking of the hall clock. She padded down the corridor towards the door of the room where Ellen slept.

There was no noise, no sound. The creature on the bed laboured silently, pulling itself by long spiked thumbs over the tumbled bedclothes. Dark leathery wings lay on its back, fine membranes folded round fingers, fantastically elongated, but as finely articulated as those on a human hand. Small eyes glowed red like tiny coals as it crept away from the sleeper's arm resting on the counterpane. A tiny slit showed on the white underside, just above the place where the veins snaked up from the wrist in fine blue tracery. This was the area the bat had chosen, slashing through the skin with incisors as sharp as razors, grooved tongue lapping the blood, the flow maintained by a powerful anticoagulant. It stopped crawling now, having sensed a disturbance. Not in this room, but somewhere in the house.

Edith Baxter opened the door and sensed nothing at all. Except that it was cold. She hugged her dressing gown to her and went over to the window. It was only open a crack, but that was enough. On a night like this, the girl could catch her death. She pulled it shut, securing the lock on the top. Just at that moment, she looked up. Something black spiralled up, whirled like a leaf between her and the street light, and was gone. The movement, odd and erratic, reminded her of bats. There were plenty of roosts over in the cemetery, but she had to be mistaken. Bats hibernate in the wintertime, surely? More likely to be dirt on her glasses. She took them off and examined the lenses. Hopelessly smeary, polishing just made them worse.

Edith Baxter tucked her granddaughter's arm back in and straightened the counterpane. In the darkness, she failed to notice the slight cut, the tiny drops of blood. The girl's hair was damp, skin slightly feverish to the touch. She moaned slightly, and her head turned on the pillow. Her eyes tracked rapidly, scanning beneath the lids, but she did not wake. She was far removed in time and place, deep in a dream in which she had become the other Ellen.

PART TWO

Fruits like honey to the throat
But poison in the blood

"Goblin Market" – Christina Rossetti

10

It was odd at first, like being two people, but after a while the separation blurred and Ellen's world became her own.

She opened her eyes to find herself in a long room with a tall ceiling. The windows were small, set high up, well above head height. There were maps on the wall and gas lamps had been lit against the gloom outside. A tall woman was wiping chalk from a free-standing blackboard. The staccato clatter of desk lids snapping shut announced that the day had ended. In silence, girls began to file out, row after row. Ellen followed the general exodus.

Outside, in the long cream and brown painted corridor, chatter swelled as the girls discussed what they intended to do over the next few days. Ellen collected her hat and coat. She spoke to no one, and no one spoke to her.

Tom was standing at the gates waiting for her.

"Ellen!"

He stepped away from the wrought-iron work where he had been leaning, arms folded. He was tall, and much better looking than Ellen had ever described him in her diary. She wondered why he was here. He had not met Ellen out of school for a long time.

He was not alone. Ellen guessed, from the way he was dressed, that his companion must be Caspar. Black hair, long and curling, rested on the collar of his rusty threadbare coat. His shirt, though clean enough, was frayed and far too large. The sleeves covered his knuckles and it hung loose at the neck. It was probably one of Tom's cast-offs. He and Tom were physical opposites. Dark and intense, Caspar barely came to Tom's shoulder. He stepped forward when he saw her, bowed in greeting, and clicked his heels.

"Hello," she said. "What are you two doing here?"

"There has been a murder, very horrible," Caspar interrupted before Tom could say anything. He spoke quickly in heavily accented, broken English. "Last night, at hospital, a woman brought in. She is woman of the streets…"

"There has been an incident," Tom said quickly. "Your father was concerned about your safety…"

"All tore about the neck she was, here and here," Caspar indicated his chest and throat, "like she been tore at by a hungry beast." He crossed himself. "If I was not here, if it was not London, England, I would think it was the work of…"

"It was a particularly vicious attack," Tom cut in, "so Doctor Laidlaw asked me to meet you. If you are ready?"

He took her bag of books, but Ellen felt a stiffness towards her, an awkwardness, that probably stemmed from the other evening. It was made more difficult by the presence of Caspar. They walked in silence for a while, the two men going on slightly ahead. Caspar did not keep quiet for long. His large brown eyes shone and flashed in his narrow-featured face as he strove to explain some complicated theory to Tom. He gestured as he spoke, using his hands and arms to do the work of the words he lacked. When they reached her gate, Ellen found herself asking them in for tea. Tom returned her books and declined, claiming other calls on his time.

Caspar looked disappointed, but followed Tom's lead in saying goodbye.

"We meet you today, tomorrow, every day. We keep you safe, Miss Ellen," he said, clicking his heels again and giving an exaggerated bow.

"Miss Ellen is on holiday now," Tom looked down at her, his face twisted into a sardonic smile, "and so will not require our services for the next couple of days. She will have other companions. Is that not right, Miss Ellen?"

Caspar shrugged, Tom's teasing sarcasm was lost on him, but Ellen was stung. She went into the house alone, slamming the door behind her.

The kitchen was steamy and rich with the smell of baking.

Mrs Dover was pouring tea for Cook and Marie. Ellen found a cup and saucer from the sideboard, helped herself to a slice of fruit cake, and sat down to join them.

The talk was of murder.

"Two carmen found her in Webb's Row. Lying outside some gates. Still warm she was – like they'd disturbed him at his work – but there was no sign of anyone about—"

"But there's nowhere to hide!" Marie exclaimed.

"There's warehouses either side..."

"When the constable came," Cook went on as if no one had spoken, "he swore he'd passed the place not a half hour before. And, what's more, he couldn't find no blood. Not a drop of the stuff, and injuries she got, it should have been running over the cobbles..."

As happens in dreams, suddenly the bright kitchen fades to a dimly lit street. Tall buildings, windows like blank eyes, rise up on either side. A woman walks alone, briefly illuminated by gas lamps too widely spaced apart. Now you see her, now you don't. She enters yet another dark space, but this one is less shadow, more an absence of light. She fails to emerge. There is no sound, just a swift movement, a bloom of crimson, and then, like a camera adjusting the aperture, a picture appears. Gaunt gates looking down. Below them, as huddled and lifeless as a bunch of rags, something lies on the ground.

Ellen started awake, trying to close down the dream she'd just had, but the last image remained as she opened her eyes and closed them again. Black against white, as if in a flash, white against black, as if in a negative. She switched on the light and glanced at the clock on the bedside table. The red digital numbers read 4:43. Hours to go until morning.

She settled back down but the light remained on; she had no wish to revisit the place she had been in that last dream. She lay for a while, trying to fight it off, but sleep returned swiftly. Her few moments of wakefulness were enough to allow the nightmare to fade and be replaced by another vision altogether different.

*　*　*

The movement of the carriage was distinctly odd, swaying from side to side as well as up and down, and there were frequent stops and starts. Ellen had not thought there might be traffic jams on the streets of Victorian London. The Count sat by her side, quiet behind his dark glasses. All the diaries had said was true, and more – he was incredibly handsome. There was something else, something the diaries had not described, a kind of dangerous stillness about him. He spoke little, but when he did, his accent, although much less pronounced, reminded her of Caspar. The Countess sat opposite. She was a large woman, powerfully built, opulently dressed in fur and silk. She reminded Ellen of an old-time opera singer. Her voice was rich and deep as she enthused about their shopping trip. Ellen turned to see that the back of the carriage was piled high with packages. All for her, it seemed.

Again she had the feeling of being two people at the same time. The other Ellen's emotions flashing on to her own. The whole experience, the buying, the goods, the shops, had left her feeling dissatisfied, vaguely unhappy.

At first, she had been dazzled by the West End, the new department stores with their huge plate-glass windows and acres of counters. The shop assistants were charming, they helped put her at ease, nothing was too much trouble. She could have anything she wanted, but novelty turned to shock at how much it was costing.

"Countess!" she had said in a fierce whisper. "I really must protest! I cannot possibly accept…"

The Countess turned with a puzzled frown, then her creamy brows cleared and she let out a laugh which echoed round the fitting room.

"You think I am paying for this?" She held up the silky stuff of a ball dress. "Oh, no, my dear! Not me, although I would, gladly. I am here to advise only. Everything is to be billed to Anton, he insists." She laughed again, more quietly this time. "So English! So proper! Your father is paying, do not worry."

One anxiety was immediately replaced by another. Why did she need so many clothes? It was as though they were collecting together a trousseau. And why so much formal evening wear? Gloves, bags, cloaks, stoles... Where on earth was she going to be wearing those? As the day went on, her worries grew, spoiling her enjoyment.

The Countess was skilled in her judgement of people. She could tell when Ellen had had enough. She whisked them off to a coffee shop tucked away behind one of the main thoroughfares. Inside was all silver and glass against the dark shine of polished mahogany. Waiters, snow-white aprons against black suits, delivered spun sugar confections to women as elegant as the cakes they consumed. Men, dashing and sophisticated, hid behind newspapers, sipping dark coffee from small china cups.

Ellen was given a huge slice of what looked like Black Forest gâteau, but one mouthful told her she had never tasted anything like it. So light it seemed to melt on the tongue, yet the taste was rich and complex. She enjoyed the first few forkfuls very much but then the flavours seemed to cloy and she felt full up. She found herself wishing for something plainer, simpler, like a buttered scone or a slice of fruit cake.

The Countess was subject to no such inhibitions. She ate greedily, working her way through a whole selection of fancy pastries. When she had finished, she dabbed delicately at the corners of her mouth, and turned to the other two members of the party. Neither of them had eaten anything at all.

"Fransz. What has happened to your appetite? And Grace," she turned to the young woman sitting opposite Ellen, "you must eat or you will waste away…"

Grace Wickham, the Countess's young lady companion, was in her early twenties. She was very pretty, many of the men in the room were eyeing her discreetly, but she was excessively slender and very pale. Her blonde hair and light blue eyes gave her an almost silver transparency. Rouge had been applied to cheeks and lips, but it only served to emphasize her pallor.

"I feel perfectly well, Countess. Don't worry about me."

"Oh, but I do, you see." The Countess purred the words and, leaning towards her, touched her on the cheek.

The gesture was affectionate but, although the young woman was careful to hide it, Ellen saw her flinch slightly and the expression that came into her eyes she recognized. It was the revulsion she herself felt at any caress from the Countess. There was something else besides. Something the dilating pupils could not disguise. Fear. The young woman's thin hand clutched convulsively, the knuckles whitening, as the Countess whispered in her ear. Her nails dug in deep enough to draw blood. Ellen noticed red crescents in the folds of white linen when Grace placed her crushed napkin on the table.

11

Ellen woke in the morning with the dream still clear in her mind. She immediately reached for the diaries, opening them at the page she had reached the day before, the place marked with a card. She flicked on until she found the name: Grace Wickham. She scanned back and forth through the pages. There could be no mistake. She had dreamt what she had not yet read. She lay back in bed and stared up at the ceiling. What could that possibly mean? It was like something out of a "Strange but True" magazine.

The feeling of strangeness did not leave her, but she soon realized that some of the symptoms were physical. Her throat was worse. It hurt to swallow and her hair was plastered to her forehead; she was covered all over with a light sweat.

She padded to the bathroom and turned on the shower. One glance in the mirror was enough. The glands in her neck were all swollen up. She looked like a panda.

A shower and a change of pyjamas made her feel

slightly better, but she decided to stay in bed for the rest of the day. Maybe that would do the trick. If she pretended she was OK, it might just go away. She knew, deep inside, that it would not, but her main fear now was that Gran would realize how bad she was and call the doctor. Or worse, call her mother. That must be avoided at all costs. Mum would make a terrible fuss, insist she was whisked off into hospital for observation. Then she wouldn't be able to see Andy again and she'd never find out what happened to Ellen.

27th February, 1878

I am writing this in bed before getting dressed. Instead of this Journal filling my empty hours, it is becoming increasingly difficult to find a spare moment to write it. I seem to have less and less time to myself.

Another shopping trip is planned, this time without the Count, our object being to purchase those things a gentleman should have no interest in. My apprehensions grow rather than diminish. What are all these clothes for? Why must I acquire a whole new wardrobe, down to petticoats and drawers? I feel plans are afoot, but Papa is being evasive. Also, I am concerned about Grace. She is near my own age and I enjoy her companionship. I have only known her a few days, but I think we have become friends. She is witty and I have much to learn from her. She has a knowledge of the world which I lack. Her health is not good, however, and she plainly loathes the Countess. Why does she stay in her employ? In some way I think the two things are connected. I am determined to speak to her about it. That is, if the Countess will leave us for five minutes together!

28th February, 1878

I have managed to speak alone with Grace and what she told me worries me even more! After half a day of tedious fitting and fussing, the Countess abandoned us in Regent Street while she went into yet another shop for yet another item she could no longer live without. We were standing opposite Burlington Arcade, enjoying the sunshine, the first hint of spring so far this winter, and I asked Grace outright – if you hate her so much, why do you stay with her?

She was staring across the street, not looking at me, and there was little humour in her laughter as she replied: "Because I don't want to end up like them."

I looked in the same direction but could see nothing special – just the usual stream of passers-by: gentlemen strollers, clerks and civil servants, women shoppers and girls in business.

"I can't see…"

"Look again."

Two women, dressed much like us, were standing on opposing sides of the Arcade entrance, stationary figures in the stream of pedestrians. One twirled her umbrella, the other looked at her watch.

"They are prostitutes."

I tried not show my shock and, I must confess, I surveyed the two with a great deal more interest.

"How can you tell?"

Grace shrugged and smiled.

"I just know. Watch."

Presently, a man approached the taller of the two. He tipped his hat and, after a moment or two's conversation, they went off together. Then, after another minute or so, the very same thing happened to the other.

"Are you sure?" I asked Grace. "They might have just been waiting…"

"I'm sure." Grace turned to examine the contents of the window behind her. "And if the Countess takes much longer, it will be our turn to be approached."

"I still don't see why it should happen to you…"

"Don't you? Well, I'll tell you. I have no friends. No family. And, other than what I can earn, no money. If I lose my position, I lose everything. To get another, I will need references. And she knows … knows things about me. I was lucky to get this job. If I leave her she will make quite certain I do not get another. I would end up like those two – if I'm lucky. If not," she gave a slight shrug, "I could be walking the streets of Whitechapel for the price of a bed. I'm better off with her," she held her high collar tighter about her throat as if against a sudden chill, "however distasteful I might find it. But you – you are different." She looked down at me, her pale eyes serious, pleading. "They are dangerous, corrupt. You must distance yourself from them. Tell your father…" She laid her gloved hands on my shoulders. "Listen to me, Ellen. Do not involve yourself further than you can possibly help…"

Before I could ask her to explain exactly what she meant, the Countess returned to sweep us off to our next destination. Grace's words, the desperation in her eyes, disturbed me and I enjoyed little of our expedition after *that. The Countess seemed to know something had passed between us and took care not to leave us together again. Like Grace, I do not trust her, but what can I do? Father will not listen, I know, and I have to do what he says. The Countess is an old and valued family friend. Her cousin is my father's honoured guest. There is a debt of obligation and, more than that, he is Father's patient. I am held as securely by duty as Grace is by her dependency.*

Ellen turned the page. The next one was blank. So was the next. Then came a short entry, undated:

These terrible murders continue. Another woman has been found – that makes three so far. Cook and Marie speak of little else. They pore over the Police Gazette, and glean every bit of street tittle-tattle (much to Mrs Dover's disapproval).

She turned to where the diary started again. The handwriting was more hurried, more careless, than she had ever seen it before. She began to read. The change of tone in the first paragraph struck her immediately.

– March, 1878

I have nothing with which to reproach myself. I have done nothing wrong. So why do I feel as though I did? I was an innocent party to any duplicity, so why am I left feeling anxious and guilty?

Last night I was supposed to go with the Count and his cousin, and Grace, of course, to see a play and then have supper. Papa thought me old enough now to go out on an evening engagement and it was a chance to wear some of my new finery. Marie helped me get ready and, when we had finished, I scarcely recognized myself. Even Marie stopped her prattle for a moment. She declared I looked a real beauty, sure to turn all the swells' heads. She finished by saying that she would not venture out at night for love nor money, and wouldn't rest easy until I was safe back – but she hoped I enjoyed myself.

The Count seemed pleased and complimented me on my appearance. Papa just stared and seemed to grow pale. When he helped me into the carriage his hand was shaking. He went with hardly a word of farewell. I thought he would see us off but he returned to the house, shutting the door behind him.

"Do not judge him too harshly," the Count said, as the driver whipped up the horses. "It is hard for a father to see his daughter grow up."

On our way into town, the Count informed me that plans had changed, we were not going to meet the Countess, she had cancelled at the last minute. I should have insisted on being taken back immediately. Father would never condone me being out with the Count alone, without a chaperone. But I didn't. I stayed silent. I let the carriage go on. That is when the evening began to go wrong.

I didn't think so at the time, I confess. To be with the Count, not shut up in his rooms, but out in the world, at night, with all of London before us, made me feel adult, sophisticated. I had never experienced such a feeling before. The fact that I knew it was not the right thing to do only made it more exciting.

97

We did not go to the theatre, as arranged. We did not go to see a play. We went to the music hall, a Palace of Varieties, a very different sort of entertainment. The Count had a box reserved as though he had planned this all along. I could see everything and everyone. The theatre was furnished in deep red and gold, lit by crystal chandeliers. Seats rose, tier on tier, balcony on balcony, and we looked down on a sea of heads and faces, people of every kind, from all stations and classes. When the lights went down, the stage lit up and all the chatter died down and that small space became the focus of everyone's attention.

I found it confusing at first, unlike anything I had ever seen: some of the performers were men dressed as women, others were women dressed as men. The rest of the audience were far more knowledgeable, calling out for their favourite artistes, joining in the choruses, shouting out catch-phrases before the person on stage had even said a word. I did not always understand what was going on, but I knew some of the songs from Marie, and I soon joined in with the riotous laughter and rapturous applause that followed act after act.

I was having so much fun, I did not want it to end but, when the lights went up, we left like everybody else. The street outside was full of people, as though the evening was just beginning, not drawing to a close. As the Count and I stepped out towards the waiting carriage, I saw Caspar, Tom's friend, coming towards us through the crowd. I called to him, and I'm sure he heard me, but he did not return my greeting, just stared for a moment and set off, very fast, in the opposite direction. I thought that odd, since I had been speaking to him just the other day, but what happened next was so unexpected, so strange, that I soon forgot about him.

I had assumed we would be going home, but that was not the case. The carriage set off through the throng and quite soon stopped. The Count handed me down and we were standing outside a restaurant, a kind of supper house. From the way he was greeted, it was plain that he was well known to the maître d'hôtel; he obviously does not spend every evening in his apartment, either entertaining me, or practising his chess. We were ushered to a private room, and a table set for two, illuminated by candles. Champagne was chilling on ice. The Count poured one glass for me. I drank it too fast, the bubbles exploding behind my nose. He poured another. The table held food I have either never tried, or do not know. Oysters have to be swallowed straight down, they taste of the sea. Caviare is sturgeon's roe, he explained, loading little triangles of toast and carrying them towards my mouth. The black eggs were glistening, glutinous, fishy tasting.

He talked of my mother, her charm, her beauty. He said I remind him of her, tonight especially.

The wine must have made me bold. I asked if he was in love with her.

"Find a man who wasn't," he said with a smile. "I was young, not much more than a boy. Believe me, it is worst at that age." His smile took on a bitter edge. "Hopeless."

The waiter cleared the table and brought fruit, figs and grapes, and a small decanter. The Count showed me how to eat a fig and poured me a tiny glass of the golden wine that tastes of flowers. I have always found it hard to guess his age; in the soft candle glow he seemed as young as he must have been when he knew my mother. All the time his eyes were on mine. Maybe it was the flickering light, but they seemed to change colour: from green, to red, to tawny tiger yellow.

When we finished eating he asked me to dance. Music came in from outside, shadowy figures flitted past, etched on frosted glass. He asked me if I would care to join them. He took me in his arms and all the awkwardness I have ever felt at dancing class dropped away from me. We moved effortlessly. I wondered why I ever thought him cold. His skin felt warm against mine, his breath hot on my neck, my bare shoulder. The world outside myself seemed to be slowing down, I grew languorous, my eyelids drooping, although I was not tired. I felt as if I was turning into liquid, as though I was melting inside.

That's it. That's all of it. We did not touch, other than as dancing partners. We did not kiss. I swear it. Nothing improper happened. So why do I feel as though it did? Also – this diary must never be read by anyone else – I feel confused, torn about inside. I know I acted unwisely, to say the least, but when I think of last night, his eyes, the candlelight, I know that I would do it again. Even if I have to lie. In fact, it is all I can do to stop myself from going to him, right now, and begging him to take me.

Ellen felt very tired and suddenly impatient with the writer. What was all the fuss about? He never even kissed her! She pushed the diary aside but, despite her annoyance, she soon picked it up again, curious to see if this other Ellen and the Count were going to get it on or not. It looked as though they might, but Victorians did not do that kind of thing, did they? She opened it to the page she had just read but the next entry marked a shift of subject. Temporarily at any rate, all thoughts about the Count seemed to have been banished.

7th March, 1878

As I write the date, I realize it is the first month of spring, but I have no sense of that season ever coming. Today has been so gloomy and foggy, it is difficult to say whether it dawned or not.

Two more bodies have been discovered. Two more women murdered. That makes five in less than two weeks. A record, even for this district. The frequency, and horrific nature of the attacks, is spreading terror through the streets, even though this community is well used to violence and viciousness. Certainly Cook and Marie have been affected by it. It is all they ever seem to talk about, and they are not alone. News is passed, word of mouth, from house to house. Newspaper reports merely go to confirm what everyone knows already. Even I can't help being drawn into the discussion as Marie outlines the peculiarities, case by case. How is it that these murders can occur in such a populous area? People live so close to each other, packed into houses, all occupied from top to bottom; the streets are never empty, day or night. Yet no one has heard as much as a shout of surprise, let alone a cry for help.

"Tears their throats out before they can utter a word," says Cook. "That's what I heard."

And what about the two women last night? According to rumour, they died within minutes of each other, but were found in separate places which are, as the crow flies, at least a mile apart.

"Maybe he can fly," Marie whispered, looking even more terrified.

This was too much – even for Cook. She told Marie to get on with her work and not be so d---ed silly.

8th March, 1878

No more murders, but the fear, and the fog, continue. Cook is worried about her old mother. She lives near the place where one of the last victims was found and is too frightened even to venture out. Cook had planned to use her afternoon off "to see her all right and take a few necessaries". She was just preparing to leave, when Papa sent a message via Mrs Dover. He is hosting a meeting of Fellows from The Royal Society and they will be staying for dinner.

Cook wanted to send Marie, but anyone could see that was going to be impossible. The very idea was enough to set Marie off wailing as though Cook had proposed pitching her directly into the path of the Monster. Mrs Dover also objected, saying if Marie could be spared from her duties, which she doubted, she was too young to go. Marie spends most of her time avoiding Dover, and the rest complaining about her, but on this occasion she was more than grateful for her intervention. On the other hand, Cook, who dislikes any kind of reminder of the Housekeeper's seniority, looked most put out and inclined to argue. So, to keep the peace, I said I would go.

They all objected to that. I pointed out, reasonably, that I am the same age as Marie, all the attacks had occurred after nightfall, it is not far, I would be back long before that. Mrs Dover's remark that it was "a bit of a rough area" brought a poisonous look from Cook. I replied that I would be quite safe. No one there will harm me. They all know who I am and nearly every family hereabouts has reason to be grateful to my father in one way or another. Anyway, Tom was around today. I had seen him, earlier, going in to see my father. He would go with me if I asked him. As if on cue, Tom came into the kitchen. He volunteered at once to go himself, but Cook was frightened that the sight of a strange young man, even a medical one, might bring on her "old Ma's condition". At length it was agreed that Tom and I would go together.

"I wanted to see you," he said, as we set off. "I came looking for you."

"Well, here I am," I replied as we went through the gates. "You've found me."

With a basket over one arm, and my cloak wrapped around me, I felt like Little Red Riding Hood. The fog had thickened even since this morning. It rolls up from the river to mix with the smoke from the chimneys and hang over everything like discoloured muslin. Lampposts and horses loomed suddenly out of streets made ghostly and flat as a photograph.

"What do you want to talk to me about?"

I pulled the cowl closer, partly to ward off the mist and its cold clammy touch, but also because I didn't want Tom to read my feelings. Recently, I know I have neglected Tom, rather than the other way round. In my secret thoughts, in my deepest heart of hearts, he is being steadily erased, replaced by the Count.

Tom started to speak, but then fell silent. I looked up. We were passing the site of the latest murder. Like everybody else, we stopped and stared. Yesterday the area was crowded, extra police had been brought in to keep the people back. Today there was just a lone constable guarding the spot, a nondescript grimy corner where one tall building met another. There was nothing to see. Any bloodstains had been washed away long since. The actual place was cordoned off by ropes but someone had reached in and put a posy of violets. Tom crossed himself, which surprised me, I did not think he was of the Catholic faith. As we went on, I asked him about it.

"No," he replied, "I am not. Something Caspar said, that's all. Made the gesture seem appropriate."

"I saw him – the other night…" I started to say, but Tom cut in.

"I know. He told me. What were you doing? Coming out of a music hall. Alone. With the Count. Does your father know about it?"

"Yes," I lied.

I did not want to argue with him, but his tone, cross and censorious, stung me.

"You have never visited such an establishment, I suppose?" I snapped.

"Yes – but…" He shook his head. "It's different for me – I'm a man."

"Oh – how is it different? There were plenty of ladies there…"

"Women, maybe. I doubt that they were ladies."

For one so young, Tom's views on men and women are hopelessly old fashioned. I was about to tell him so, when he stopped me.

"I am concerned, that's all. Don't let's quarrel." He shrugged and sighed. "If your father knows, and approves, it's hardly my place…" His mouth set in a grim line, "Especially now."

"Why especially now?"

He was about to say more but we were hard by the court where Cook's mother lives.

"It will wait," he said, "until we have completed our errand."

"What is it, Tom?" I asked as we came out. "What did you want to tell me?"

He paused, as though what he had to say was especially difficult.

"Your father and I have had a – disagreement. I am to complete my training at the London Hospital. He does not wish to continue as my tutor."

"A disagreement?" I was so shocked all I could think to do was repeat his words – like a parrot. "What about?"

"I can't tell you that." He reached in his pocket and brought something out. "Caspar has asked me to give you this. He asked me to make sure you wear it."

I looked down. He was offering me a crucifix.

"What on earth for?"

"It has to do with the Count. He saw you two together the other night and he recognized him. When I mentioned the Count's family name he grew most alarmed. He called him something in his own language. A Vampyr. Undead. Some species of ghost, or creature, that preys on others, sucking their blood…"

"What?"

I could hardly believe my ears. Caspar must have taken leave of his senses and Tom with him. Tom of all people. I had always considered him aptly named; now Doubting Thomas was talking about spectres from peasant *superstition and penny gothic novels, as though they were walking in our midst and real.*

"How can you believe such things? You are a man of science…"

"Caspar is also a man of science," Tom replied. "In his country such things are known and recorded. There is documentary evidence that these — creatures — actually do exist and he is convinced that this Count is one of them. He has relatives in the country — where he comes from. It is not as he has told it to you. The whole country, for miles and miles around, is a wasteland. Now he has moved out, to seek fresh victims, fresh blood — and where better than this?"

He indicated the warren of streets around us.

"What are you saying?" I felt myself go cold as if ice was pouring down my back. "That these — these murders — are the Count's doing?"

"I do not know. Caspar thinks so. But we need more proof than we have at the moment."

"You speak as though you are investigating this."

I started to laugh. Tom and Caspar made an unlikely pair of detectives.

"Don't laugh. It's not funny."

"Isn't it? It beats anything I saw at the music hall. I think you are both quite crazy."

"All right," Tom sighed. "You don't have to believe me. But wear this." He held out the crucifix. "Please. Wear it for both of us."

He looked so sincere and worried that I had to accept.

I took it from him. It was a fine piece, and looked old. The ivory figure was beautifully carved, the silver cross heavy and substantial. I slipped the long chain over my head.

"Very well," I said. "If it will make you happy."

Mrs Dover was glad to see me back safe and sound but the relief on her face was soon replaced by another expression, one I had seen several times lately: puzzled, even angry, as though I have done something to upset her. I cannot think what it could be, so I asked her again: "What is the matter?" She held her head in the special way she has when she doesn't approve of something, and said that it was not her place to say, I had best ask my father. I reply that I will. I have several matters I wish to speak to him about, not least the way he has treated poor Tom, but I am told his guests have already arrived. My questions will have to wait until tomorrow.

12

"Weather like this, bed's the best place for you," Edith Baxter remarked as she brought in a tray of food.

Ellen glanced out of her window. The curtains framed a day as dismal as the one described in the diaries. She left her lunch untouched. She did not feel like eating at all. Her grandmother had prepared tomato soup, and little triangles of bread and butter. Even looking at it made her feel sick. She put the tray down by the side of the bed and picked up the diary.

9th March, 1878

This morning I went to seek Papa at the earliest opportunity. I found him hard at work in his laboratory, preparing slides to study under the microscope. He does not like to be disturbed when he is working, and was not best pleased to see me, but I had waited long enough. I wanted to know why he had treated Tom so unfairly.

"He questioned my clinical judgement," he said without looking up, "and then went on to make vile accusations against a man who is both my patient and a guest in my house."

"You mean the Count?"

"Yes. What has he been telling you?"

I recounted my conversation with Tom. Papa did not know about my excursion to the music hall, so I left out the part about the crucifix.

"I am surprised at Tom." Father rose from his bench and began pacing. "Very surprised indeed. I thought his mind ran on opposite lines. I would have credited him with a lack of imagination, if anything. I have always found him thorough to the point of plodding and yet he comes here expecting me to take the ravings of some half-baked foreigner seriously."

"What Caspar said – about the Count…"

"Superstitious nonsense."

"But…"

"I will not hear another word!" He held up his hand to cut me off. "I have fought superstition all my life. If you recall, I was hounded from my last appointment by backward-thinking bigots." He gestured his impatience. "Twenty years ago cholera, typhoid, were thought to result from evil humours, poisonous miasmas. Now we know they are caused by germs, microbes, organisms smaller than the eye can see, borne by water. Thousands would be dying even now if we had stuck to the old beliefs. No," he shook his head, "there is a purely scientific explanation. The Count is suffering from a rare blood disease. Come here and I'll show you."

He beckoned me over to his microscope.

"Look."

He slipped in a slide and adjusted the focus.

"That is normal, healthy blood. You see the little round cells? Those are the red blood corpuscles. See how they are perfectly round and concave?"

I nodded. He took out that slide, replacing it with another.

"This is the Count's blood before my treatment began. See how few red corpuscles there are, and the ones that are there, can you see their pathology?"

Indeed I could. The small discs were widely spaced out, and not round at all. Some were oval, some sickle-shaped, their colour decayed.

"Now look at this. A sample I took just after treatment began, and one taken yesterday."

He put in two more slides. They showed a remarkable improvement. The last showed no differences from the healthy blood I had seen a moment ago.

"As you see, it is a purely medical matter, just like any other. The Count, I am glad to say, is on his way to a full recovery. All this talk of vampires – dangerous rubbish!" He shook his head. "Tom of all people!" He looked at me then and his expression softened. "I know you are fond of the boy, and I have not discouraged your friendship with him. Indeed at one time I rather hoped … but perhaps this – rupture – is for the best. I have something to tell you, Ellen."

He stood opposite me, leaning on the bench, and outlined a future which had no place for Tom in it. When he had finished, I was so stunned, I could think of nothing to say. He knew me well enough not to take my silence for agreement and sent me to my room to consider. He wants my answer tomorrow.

10th March, 1878

I write my diary to fill my mind, to take my thoughts away from what I will say to Father.

Papa wishes me, more than that, he has decided, that I will accompany the Count and Countess to the Continent. That is why all the clothes, the new wardrobe. That is why Dover's discomfort — she knows! I am to live with them, go with them. To travel, see the world. He sees it as a great opportunity.

He says his work, at the hospital, in his laboratory, means that he cannot devote the time to me he would like. But I am quite happy with things as they are. I know he is busy. I do not feel that he is neglecting me. He shook his head when I said this, saying I still didn't understand. I am growing up and he feels that he cannot give me, living in the way that we do, the training a young lady would require if she is to be introduced to society.

I failed, for a moment, to understand him. What society? What is he talking about? Balls and débutantes? He knows that is not what I want. I do not care for "society". I want to be a doctor. I have no interest in anything else. Not now. Not ever. It is all I've ever wanted. I turned away so he could not see the tears that began to prick my eyes, and return now as I write. He has always encouraged my dreams, my desires. I thought that is what he wanted too, I thought we were agreed upon it.

He saw my reaction and came to me, turning my head towards him. I did not have to explain, he understood the source of my unhappiness. He had an answer for that, too. The medical schools in Berne, Paris, Geneva, Berlin, all accept women as a matter of course. The training there is first class, the work being carried out new and exciting. This is where the future of medical science lies. London, Edinburgh, are backwaters in comparison. If he had his time again this is where he would be going. He is offering me, his only child, a great opportunity.

I could tell by his eyes that he had made up his mind. More than that, he genuinely believes he is acting in my interest. So whether I agree, or disagree, is unimportant. Discussion is redundant. Argument, pointless. That is when I left him to seek refuge in my room.

Some instinct tells me that this is not his idea. Why? I don't know, but I am sure the Countess is behind this. I will not go! I will not do what they want, even for Papa! I will not! For a clever man he really can be very, very stupid. Either that, or he is in her thrall. The way he looks at her, talks of her – but no, that can't be so—

I look up from my diary to turn up the lamp, I can hardly see to write. The fog outside is deepening towards night. It has condensed, finer than rain on the window pane; each little drop running down contains a cargo of soot. The only things visible are the black branches of trees which look as if they will never again bear leaves. Perhaps, after all, it has nothing to do with the Countess. Perhaps it is just that he would be better off without me. I am a worry, a distraction, preventing him from giving his work his undivided attention. It is as simple as that. My anger subsides and dissolves into a gloom as deep as the day outside. He sees it as being for my own good but, in the end, everything we do has a selfish motive.

12th March, 1878

7:30 a.m. I was too dispirited yesterday even to write in

my diary. It is all planned. I am to go with them. My objections were brushed aside as silly childishness. Why is it that they want you to be grown up, responsible – until you disagree – then you are a child again.

Later. It is evening. My watch has stopped so I do not know the time. I want to write this down while it is fresh in my mind. Tom met me from school. We had a long talk. Father's actions have rather forced his hand. Tom told me of his feelings, how much he cares for me. All the distance between us disappeared and I felt closer to him than ever before. I do not know how I will accomplish it, how I can go against Father's wishes, but I will not go abroad with the Count and Countess. I have always detested her, and now the time I spent with the Count seems like the noxious goblin fruit Miss Rossetti describes. Sweet to the tongue but poisonous to the spirit. Tom and Caspar are still watching. Their detective work could prove to be our salvation. If they can prove something against him, then we can go to Father and he will have to listen.

13th March, 1878

Papa is taking us to the Opera. Myself, the Countess and Grace. The Count is "too fatigued"…

Their carriage has arrived, I just heard it coming down the drive and I must get ready.

I had to hurry, but I thought I looked reasonably presentable. When I went to greet the Countess, however, she sprang away from me with a grimace of distaste.

"Oh, no, my dear, you cannot wear that!"

I looked down, puzzled. The gown I wore was one she had selected herself, but it was not my dress she was staring at.

"It is not right. It is not – suitable. Anton, please. What do you think?"

My father, looking very handsome in evening dress, came to her assistance.

"This – this thing, about her neck…"

The Countess gestured towards the crucifix, but was careful not to touch it.

My father smiled and stroked his beard.

"Why, Ellen," he sounded amused, "what has happened? Have you undergone a conversion?"

"No, I…"

"Take it off! I have something more suitable."

She left us with a rustle of countless layers of satin and silk. My father shrugged and removed the cross from around my neck.

"Here. This is for you. A gift." She handed me a flat leather-covered box. "Very old, very valuable. I understand from Anton that soon it will be your birthday."

I endured her kiss, hot on my cheek, with the best grace I could muster.

"Open it!"

I did as instructed. The satin lid bore a worn coat of arms and the name: St Petersburg. Underneath, on black velvet silk, creased and threadbare with age, lay a necklace. It appeared to be a heraldic beast of some kind, half turned back on itself, green eyes staring out, spewing fire.

"It is emblem of my family." The Countess was

114

already fixing it about my neck. "Come. Let me show you."

She led me to the mirror over the mantelpiece and stood to the side as I gazed at myself. The necklace was certainly very fine, and of cunning design, but it fitted uncomfortably close about my throat and I found the effect, to say the least, unsettling. The stones, glowing red in the candlelight, seemed curiously transparent. It was as if someone had pricked the design into my skin and the resulting beads of blood had described a dragon.

"It is very – generous of you, Countess," I began to say, "but I have my own garnets…"

"Garnets?" The Countess rolled the word in her mouth. "You think these garnets?" Her laugh, deep and rich, resonated like a heavy bell. "The eyes are emerald, and the rest rubies. Each one unique. Matchless. It is," she searched for the correct term, "an heirloom. For many centuries, it has been in my family. Now I give it to you…"

I was even more appalled on hearing this. I did not want to own such a valuable thing. Besides, I didn't like it. I didn't like the feel of it.

"Oh, no," I started to say, "I couldn't possibly accept…"

"But you must." Her face was near to me now, her dark blue eyes glittering, almost black, like pieces of jet. "To refuse would be to insult. In my country, to reject a gift is to reject the giver. We are proud people, quick to take offence." The last word hissed from her smiling mouth. "So – it is yours. I will hear no more. Come. Let us join the others."

❈   ❈   ❈

We viewed the opera from a box. I sat next to Grace, who looked exquisite, her porcelain paleness dramatic against the black silk of her dress, and the velvet choker at her neck. She looked so beautiful that some of the gentlemen opposite seemed to have their glasses permanently trained on her rather than the stage. Nevertheless she seemed restless, fidgeting through the overture.

"I must talk to you," she whispered, as soon as the singing from the stage was sufficiently loud to drown her words.

There was no opportunity for conversation during the performance. The first time we were alone together was in the cloakroom.

"What's wrong?" I asked.

"You have to get away from them," she said as we waited for the Countess's fur to be brought.

"We have talked about this before. I told you then. It is impossible."

"You have to. Before they do this to you."

She pulled the ribbon round her neck down slightly to expose two puncture marks, angry and red.

I had never seen such injuries before.

"You should see my father…"

Her teeth showed sharp as her brittle laugh cut me off.

"I am beyond any help he might be able to bring. But you… You must not go with them. Not under any circumstances."

"What can I do? It is already decided," I replied.

I did not tell her of my idea about discrediting the Count. I did not know how far I could trust her and, I realized, I was becoming resigned. The plan I'd hatched with Tom seemed hopeless even in my eyes.

"Go to your father. You must implore him, persuade him – do anything! But do it soon. There is no time to lose!" Her pale blue eyes were on me now, pleading, agonized. "He obviously cares for you – surely he will relent? If he knew the truth about those two, he would never let you go." She shuddered. "It would be like putting a lamb into the care of a pair of tigers."

"What about you?"

"I – I have to go." The animation faded from her face, taking her loveliness with it. The light left her eyes, leaving them blank, almost colourless. "I have no choice. I told you."

"Yes, you have." I do not know what made me do it, I rarely act on impulse, but even as the words were forming in my mouth, I was unfixing the ruby necklace. "Here. Take this. Sell it. Take it to a jeweller's – in Bond Street or somewhere – and don't let them cheat you, it is very valuable. Take her coat. It's sable. Sell that as well – it should be enough to establish you, in a small way at least."

"I have no money, not even cab fare…"

I dug into my evening bag and found the sovereigns Papa had given me for pocket money.

"That should be enough for a night's lodging."

"How am I to get out of here? She will be waiting…"

Just then the attendant arrived with our cloaks. I asked if there was a back way out of the Opera House. My friend had a gentleman admirer, I explained, whom she wished to avoid. The girl smiled. One glance at Grace was enough for her to believe my story. She was used to dealing with "gentlemen pests". She showed us the service entrance.

"Good luck," I said, as Grace turned to go.

"And you." Grace gave me a hug of farewell. "I don't know how I can ever thank you…"

"There's no need." I kissed her on the cheek. "Go – quickly!"

I fastened my own cloak high round my neck, hoping the Countess would notice nothing amiss, and returned with a story about queues and crush and general mix-up.

"Grace is still waiting for your fur and her wrap," I finished. "She will be out presently."

Eventually it became clear, to the Countess at least, that she had been given the slip. Her reaction was curious. I thought she would be angry but she shrugged her large shoulders and turned her hands up in a gesture of resignation, complaining bitterly to my father about the way she had been betrayed, deceived by a common little thief. He suggested calling a constable, the coat was valuable, its theft should be reported, but she was quick enough to discourage that. There was little else to be done, so he went to call a cab, leaving us alone. She said nothing to me, but I could tell she was seething. She regarded me with narrowed eyes. It was the kind of look a cat might give when suddenly deprived of an item of prey it had been mauling.

Grace is right, there is little time to lose. While we were out, someone had been busy getting travelling trunks down from the attic. They are stacked outside my room. They are covered in fading labels. Paris, Ostend, Baden-Baden. They must have belonged to my mother.

The Countess left almost immediately, claiming fatigue as her excuse, but I could see she was still *discomfited by her companion's defection. At least Grace will be safe. Accomplishing that has halted the sapping resignation I felt earlier in the evening. I must look to myself now. I write while I wait. I have a new plan, but whether it will work or not, only time will tell. Something is urging me to record it all – now – in case I don't come back. If I am to escape the fate Grace was hinting at, if I am to convince my father, if I am to have proof, I can't just sit and wait, I have to help Tom get it.*

From this window, I can observe the front and side of the house. Tom is down there, keeping watch as he said he would. I saw him from the cab. The Countess and my father, on the other side of the cab, failed to notice him hiding in the shadows. He is waiting for the Count to come out and, when he does, Tom will follow.

I have changed into sensible boots and a plain dark walking habit. In a moment I will go and join him. I have just one more thing to put on and I am ready. I have it, safe in my evening bag, Caspar's crucifix.

And that was it. Pages and pages, blank, to the end. The rest of it must be in the next volume. Ellen went to sit up and fell back. She was feeling pretty fatigued herself. The book slipped from her grip. In fact, she was feeling pretty awful, too feeble even to get out of bed. She lay for a moment or two gathering her strength. This was ridiculous. It was mind over matter. All will-power.

Ellen managed to pull the trunk out from under the bed and to find the next diary. Maybe she stood up too quickly. She was on her feet for all of ten seconds, and unconscious before her head hit the carpet.

13

Ellen was back in bed. Gran stood looking down, lips compressed, hands fluttering in vague gestures of worry and anguish.

"I should never have allowed you to go out with Andrew. And last night – I should have made sure you got to bed early. If anything happens – goodness knows what Stella will say... I for one will never forgive myself."

"Don't, Gran. Don't phone Mum. She'll only lay a guilt trip on you. And I'll be all right." Ellen broke off. She couldn't even convince herself. Even speaking this much hurt her throat and started her coughing. "I don't want you to feel like that." She went on as soon as she had recovered. "You did right to let me go out. You gave me a day I won't forget. Look." She leaned back now, eyes closed. "I'm not stupid. I don't know how much life I've got left, all I'm asking for is the chance to live whatever there is of it. OK?"

"Yes, I suppose so."

Edith Baxter came over to the bed and gave her

granddaughter a hug, fierce and strong. Then she stood up, polishing her glasses furiously before dabbing at her cheeks with her lace-bordered handkerchief.

"Hand me a tissue, will you?" She sniffed. "This hanky's really for show, it's not quite up to it." She put her glasses back on and looked down at Ellen. "What a silly old fool I am. You don't need this, do you? There's you, all brave and dry-eyed, and me with runnels all down my powder, I shouldn't wonder. What a sight to greet the doctor."

"Doctor?"

"I had to call her, love. You were spark out on the floor, I didn't know what else to do..."

As if on cue the doorbell rang.

"That's probably her now."

Gran's GP was brisk and efficient. Her touch was gentle, her examination unhurried and thorough. Ellen gave her ten out of ten for her bedside manner – she did her very best to reassure – but, when she left, Ellen turned her face to the wall. She did not have to be told. She could tell by the careful way they closed the door. She did not have to hear the familiar mutter of ominous conversation. She was relapsing. There was no point in pretending any longer. The treatment she was in affected her immune system, so even if it was just a cold she had, or flu, it could be many times more serious for her than for other people.

"I've phoned her mother," Gran was saying. "She should be here soon."

"Good. I'll phone the hospital," the doctor replied, "warn them to expect her. Meanwhile..."

*   *   *

Ellen seemed to wake in a different age, yet she knew she was dreaming. She could see herself, standing by Tom, and be inside herself at the same time, as dreamers can. Tom was not pleased to see her. He was pleading with her to go back, when Ellen heard it. Footsteps. One light and quick. The other heavy, slower, crunching the gravel. She put a finger to Tom's lips. The Count, followed by Ivan the faithful. They must hurry. For someone "fatigued" he was moving quickly.

Gas lights flared sickly yellow through the rags of fog still blowing about. They walked along, arm in arm, saying nothing, intent on the figures, one big, one small, walking in front of them.

Two women, leaving the open door of a corner public house, nearly crashed straight into them.

Their faces were lined by harsh lives and poverty. Ellen found it impossible to tell their ages.

"What you looking at?"

The challenge had stayed the same from then until now. Ellen caught a blast of gin, as one of them leered towards her, and then Tom pulled her away. They plunged on into the darkness in pursuit of the Count.

There were few people around. Those still about were in groups of two and three; nobody wanted to be caught on their own in streets being stalked by a monster. But there will always be a few who are forced out alone, by circumstance or necessity. On the other side of the long narrow road, a woman hurried along, head down, shawl held tightly round her.

Tom dodged into a doorway, taking Ellen with him. Opposite, something moved in the deep shadows of a courtyard entrance. The woman started in terror and looked up into the face of the Count.

"Please! Sir! I have to get to the Hospital. My child is very sick. He needs medicine…"

She held up an empty bottle as if to prove her story but the Count seemed not to hear. His gloved hand was already turning her face to the side, exposing the neck to him. Even at this distance, Ellen could see his eyes, little pin points of red light. His mouth opened, the gape huge, reptilian, the two canine teeth seemed to grow and elongate, glinting like bone blades, razor-edged.

He was just about to strike when Ellen became aware of another figure standing beside him, huge, bear-like. A massive hand gripped the Count's shoulder, and a voice said, its English fractured and broken: "Go your ways, little mother. Speak of this to nobody!"

The woman seemed to wake as if from a trance. She set off down the street at a run, as though from an encounter with the devil himself, never to know why he had let her go. Ellen herself could only guess at the reason for Ivan's intervention. In his eyes the woman was good, respectable. There were plenty of the other kind around. Let his master prey on one of them. This woman, rushing to care for her son, did not deserve the terrible fate the Count had in store for her.

Tom had seen enough, more than enough.

The street eerily quiet now, deserted. Then, from the other end came the sound of talking, laughing. Two women, perhaps the two she had bumped into, were coming their way, talking loudly, defying the silence. One of them called out and a man's voice replied, jocular but stern.

"Get on home, the pair of yer. Don't you know there's a maniac about?"

The two women howled with laughter. Tom closed his eyes. His prayer had been answered.

"It's a constable. Just across the street," he whispered. "I'll go and get him. You stay here."

He had been gone moments. He was just yards away, in the middle of the road, walking towards the officer, when she sensed something behind her. In the doorway, a column, blacker than the shadows around it, was rising from the floor. Before it even took shape, she heard the voice of the Count, whispering to her.

"Ellen! What a surprise! So you wish to be my companion of the night? Welcome! It will be my pleasure!"

She smelt leather as a hand went over her mouth, and heard the rustle of silk as he took her under his cloak. She heard Tom's voice, saying, "I have a female companion. She's right here…"

She did not see the policeman's puzzled look as he stared into the empty doorway. All sound had died away, and with it all sight. There was only darkness.

Ellen woke to hear her mother's voice arguing with someone.

"No, I am afraid you cannot. She is very ill. Very ill indeed – thanks to you."

"I'm sorry. I didn't realize… I mean she seemed perfectly all right…"

"Who is it?"

Gran was sitting in the chair by the bed. How long had she been there? Ellen had no idea. She had lost all track of time.

"It's Andrew. Stella is giving him rather a difficult time by the sound of it."

"Can I see him?"

Ellen went to get up and found even moving that much brought her out in drenching sweat.

"I don't think so, dear."

Her grandmother's eyes flicked to the window. In the distance, an ambulance siren waxed and waned, beating through the streets, getting nearer. Ellen knew it was coming for her. Sure enough, the sound died outside the house.

"Gran?"

"Yes?"

She came over to her granddaughter. The girl was so weak she could hardly hear her.

"You know those diaries – the ones I'm reading?"

Edith Baxter frowned and bent near. Already from the street came the sound of feet jumping down, the rattle and clatter as the ambulance men released the stretcher.

"Make sure Andy gets them. That's what he has come for. I said I'd let him read them. It's important…"

"I'll see he gets them. Don't you worry."

"Promise!"

"Of course! I promise!"

Edith Baxter was perplexed by the urgency of the request, but she would do her very best to fulfil it. How could she refuse? The grey eyes, looking up into her own, were pleading, beseeching, as if the child's very life depended on it.

14

The next part was a nightmare. Ellen slipped in and out of consciousness and, as she did so, she seemed to pass from her own life into that of another.

She was wrapped and strapped and then carried downstairs. The metal bars on the side of the stretcher were put up to stop her rolling off. Once she was outside, the sensation of being carried became exaggerated. She seemed to seesaw in the air, and the shouts of the ambulance men became gulls calling. When she put out her hands, the rough wool blanket seemed to have turned to satin. She opened her eyes and could see nothing. She was in a closed box. Then she realized. It was not a box, it was a coffin.

She fought to free herself, but her arms seemed to be tied down.

"Steady on, love," a voice above her said, "just fixing this. It might hurt just a little bit. There, that's it."

The ambulance man attached the intravenous drip to a stand.

"Soon have you there. Don't worry. Soon have you better, you'll see…"

His presence signalled Ellen's return to her real life in her own world. She relaxed and let his cheerful chant of reassurance calm her down.

The relief was short lived. Even as he held her hand she felt herself slipping away from him. She was being carried again, this time manhandled and none too gently. There was the sound of shouting and many feet running. When they set her down the motion became that of a ship, she could even hear the lapping of the water.

The lid opened and the light was blinding. She could see nothing for some moments but, when she could focus, she recognized the face looking down at her. There was something covering the lower part, something which puffed in and out.

The strong light diffused into something altogether gentler. She sat up and seemed to swim into a room, low-ceilinged and compact, but luxuriously furnished.

"Ah, Ellen. None the worse for your unorthodox entry on to our splendid vessel." The Count looked down at her, the scarf, or whatever it was, gone from his mouth. "It is a black schooner, swift and streamlined. The captain and crew I picked myself. I apologize for the inconvenience, but you have brought this on yourself by your excessive curiosity."

The Count offered his hand, but Ellen refused his help, preferring to climb out by herself.

"Do not be afraid…"

"I am not afraid," Ellen replied firmly, although she was. Very.

"You will not be harmed. In fact, Elizabetta and I

admire your courage, your bravery. Many men would not for their life do what you have done tonight."

"You must let me go! You cannot keep me here like this! I will be missed!"

The Count smiled.

"May I ask by whom, exactly?"

"By my father. Mrs Dover."

"As far as they know, you are sleeping soundly. And when they find otherwise – our ship is swift." He made a motion with his long bony hands, like a fish. "We will be far from here. Even now they are casting off from the shore, the ship is preparing to sail. Can you not hear?"

From above came the rhythmic shout of many men hauling on ropes.

"The sailors, the captain…"

She knew the answer to that before the words were out of her mouth.

"No one saw you come aboard. Only the coffin of our poor, dear niece, Elena. To die so young, so beautiful, such a tragedy! To carry her back to her homeland is our sad duty. No. You cannot escape. You must remain. As our guest. Or…" He gestured towards the coffin. "The captain and his crew carry a body on board. They expect to carry one off again. Perhaps we arrange a burial at sea." He shrugged. "It is your choice."

"I do not understand. How can I be your guest? You can't keep me here as a guest and prisoner at the same time –that's impossible."

"Not our prisoner." The Countess emerged from the adjoining cabin. "You would not be prisoner. As Fransz says, we offer you a choice. We offer you more. Eternal life. You will never die. You can be like us!" The Countess was approaching, undulating towards her, the oily silk of her many skirts rustling like dead snake skins. "You must listen, my dear. To refuse means your death – so – attend carefully. We chose you, not at random, you understand. We chose you because of your dear dead mother." Her glistening eyes seemed to dim for a moment, as though tears came into them. "My darling Isobella. She was near, so near to joining us, but then she became pregnant. Carrying a child interfered somehow. Maybe one blood fights another." Her spread hands, splayed wide, showed pale palms, devoid of lines. Many rings bit into the thickness of her fingers. "Who knows? But – she died, giving you life. Now we give to you what she could not have."

She was near now. Ellen instinctively shrank back. One hand went to her breast.

"Do not be alarmed," the Countess added, mis-interpreting her retreat for fear. "The process is painless. You will die from this life into another. Once the transition is complete, you will wonder at any reluctance you had. You are made to be one of us! Believe it!" Ellen felt the chill of her touch. "I know you took my Grace from me, but still I am not angry." She smiled, wide so Ellen could see the long canines. "Such cleverness! So much spirit! You will make a perfect vampire!"

Ellen had been right. They had been keeping her for something. She was not to be an ordinary victim. She was to be one of them. Once she was away from her father, they could do with her as they liked. Once she was initiated, she would forget her old life and grow into another. She would be a willing partner, being like them, feeding like them. "All tore about the neck she was":

Caspar's words came back and she shuddered. To be a vampire. Undead. For lifetime after lifetime. For ever.

The Countess held out her left arm, the underneath plump and white, naked to the shoulder. With the long thumbnail on her right hand, she released a hidden catch on the massive ring that she wore on the middle finger. The stone snapped back to reveal another, a black pyramid, each oblique edge as sharp as a razor. She pierced the skin where blue veins marbled her wrist. Dark blood began to well. She held herself with care, in order not to spill, and offered it up to Ellen.

"Come. Drink." Her voice was soft and silky. "One drop and you will never want anything but this."

Beneath her dress, Ellen's fingers had found the hard outline of the crucifix. In frantic haste she tore through the thin material and held it out. The Countess was so near, the crucifix touched her. There was a hiss, then the sickening smell of burning flesh. Her blue-black eyes bulged, suddenly cloudy, opaque with fear. Her mouth opened in a shriek of agony as the sign of the cross seared itself, puckered and red, into her forearm.

Ellen turned towards the Count who had been prowling near, like some secondary predator. He leapt back, knocking over the table. The lamp fell and smashed. Oil spilled out, igniting and spreading towards the Countess in a crooked ribbon of fire. Her screams became one continued high-pitched note as the flames caught greedily at the hem of her dress and spread on to the many layers of petticoats that lay beneath the crinoline gown.

The Count did not even glance at his cousin, he kept his eyes firmly on Ellen. Terror held her for a moment more, then she began stepping backwards. He was gaining on her, mirroring her every movement. She was still clutching the crucifix but knew she would have to turn when she reached the door. Her hand found the handle. One swift movement, and she was through and out in the corridor.

The release from his eyes made her feel light-headed, but the respite was only temporary. There was no way of securing the door from this side and she had no key. Already the handle was turning when a voice behind her said:

"Come, little sister. Come with me."

Ivan picked her up and carried her to the companion-way. Ellen had no time to wonder why he had intervened, she was just grateful that the code he lived by somehow impelled him to defy the Count and save her. Once on deck, he slammed down the cover and, picking up a loaded packing case as if it was a matchbox, threw it down on top.

"Fire! Fire!" he yelled at the startled seamen. "That way blocked."

Wisps of smoke were beginning to creep round the edge of the hatch. Shouts of command rang out and the sailors dispersed in frantic activity.

"Come, Miss Ellen. Still not safe."

Ivan took her to the side of the ship and threw her off.

It seemed to take a long time for Ellen to reach the water. Part of her mind noticed that the fog had gone, moonlight made a bright path across the river. The fire had broken through to the deck and a red glow was adding itself to the glittering surface. She heard a strange concert of squeaking and squealing and tiny bodies hurtled past her.

Some, already balls of flame, hissed as they hit the water. The rats, panicked by the spreading fire, were leaving the vessel.

The water was icy cold. She plunged beneath the little lapping waves and all light was extinguished. She continued to fall, on and on, into the blackness, her heavy clothes, waterlogging quickly, dragging her down. She knew she should struggle, swim back to the surface, but suddenly the water did not feel cold any more; the darkness seemed velvety, almost cosy. She no longer wanted to fight. Something grabbed her, yanking on her arm. She tried to pull away. She wanted to stay here. It was so much easier just to curl up and drift with the darkness wrapped all around her like a blanket.

Suddenly there was the most terrible pressure on her chest. She heard a voice, somewhere above her. It sounded like Tom.

"One, two, three," he was shouting. "Stand clear!"

And then there was the terrible pressure again, spreading out from her chest, racking her entire body. Again and again, it happened. Why couldn't he leave her alone? What was he doing here?

"She's breathing. I can feel a pulse. Oh, thank God!"

Ellen opened her eyes at last, expecting to see Tom. Somehow he had been on the river, somehow he had got to her. But she was not in a boat, or on water. The light was glaring and neon. There were machines bleeping around her. Her fingers gripped crisp white sheets. She was in hospital. The man looking down at her was a doctor.

He pulled the mask from his face, and she could see that

he was a stranger. Relief flooded through her, because, just before he did that, she could have sworn that the eyes looking into hers were those of the Count.

There were tubes in her mouth, down her throat; she could not speak, or breathe on her own, but even that reassured her. This was not a dream, however frightening it might be. She was not waking into some endlessly repeated nightmare. She was back in the actual world, her own world, back in reality.

PART THREE

The blood is the life

Deuteronomy 12:23

PART THREE

15

"Hello, Ellen. My name's Jenny, Jenny Cheung. How are you feeling today?"

The question came from a nurse standing beside her bed.

"I'm OK. I think."

Ellen had not been awake long enough to really know.

The nurse returned her weak smile with warmth and humour. She was young, not very much older than Ellen herself, and very pretty, with creamy clear skin and slanting eyes which, Ellen noted with surprise, were grey, not black or brown. Her shiny dark hair was pinned neatly back under her cap. She wore the belt of an SRN and her uniform was immaculate.

"You look better than you did last night. Let's just see…"

Jenny took the chart from the end of the bed.

"You'll do," she said, after completing her checks. "Temperature down, pulse rate regular, blood pressure near normal." The relief was clear on her face. "You had us worried," she added, as she swabbed Ellen's arm and prepared to take a blood sample. "Look away if it makes you feel queasy."

Ellen eyed the large syringe and obeyed. It always made her feel weird, seeing her blood being drawn out that way, no matter how many times they did it to her.

"There."

Ellen felt the slight sting of spirit, and a Band Aid being applied.

"All over."

"Just one thing," Ellen said as the nurse labelled the sample. "My chest hurts."

"I'm not surprised. You nearly died. They had to get the CRASH team. Hey, it's OK…"

Jenny sat down on the bed and took her hand. It's one thing to recognize in theory that you might die at any time, but to have been that close and not even know… Ellen felt tears of fear and self-pity well up and spill over.

"You're doing fine now. Really well. It's over!"

Once she started, she was too weak to stop. Jenny held her in her arms. She smelt faintly of fresh flowers, as well as clean starched material and hospital disinfectant. Eventually Ellen broke away, snuffling. How stupid can you get? Sobbing on the shoulder of a complete stranger. She looked round for tissues but the drip in her wrist made it difficult to reach. Tears threatened again. Ellen lay back on the pillows. This was impossible.

"Here." Jenny took a tissue from the box and dried her eyes. "Don't apologize. We all need a good cry. You can do the same for me sometime. Blow. That's it. Feel better?"

Ellen nodded. Again, she noticed her eyes. They really were startling.

"I'm sorry, I didn't mean to stare…"

Jenny smiled. "That's OK. My father is Chinese, but my mother is English. Now. We'd better get you sorted out. Looking your best. Dr Stacey will be round in a minute."

Ellen submitted quietly as Jenny sponged her face and combed her hair. She hated this. Hated being so helpless, but at least Jenny was patient and kind. Her touch was gentle but firm and all the time she worked she chatted, trying to make Ellen feel at ease, normal again. Jenny's father was from Hong Kong, her mother from Birmingham. Her family ran a Chinese wholesale supermarket there, but she had moved to London to complete her training. She now lived in a small flat with her cousin above a family restaurant. She helped out sometimes when they were very busy. Did Ellen like Chinese food?

Who didn't?

"When you have recovered, I'll cook something really special. Now, how do you feel?"

Ellen looked in the hand-mirror Jenny held for her. She looked a wreck, but a tidy wreck, and she felt much better. In the looking glass, Jenny returned her smile and Ellen knew she had found a friend. She had spent enough time in hospitals to know that, despite the brisk efficiency and superficial friendliness, they could be lonely places. The hours could seem very long between one visiting time and another and each change in shift meant a different set of faces.

"What's he like? Dr Stacey?" Ellen asked. "I don't think I've seen him before, he's not one of my usual doctors."

"He was here last night when you came in and has

agreed to take your case. He's from the States. He has a fantastic reputation in the field. You're very lucky…"

Jenny busied herself, tidying the bed. As she talked about him, the words came too quickly, as though rehearsed. Ellen sensed a certain lack of conviction.

"But you don't like him?"

Jenny shrugged and looked away.

"It's not for me to say… He gets very good results, excellent recovery rate—"

"Thank you, nurse."

Jenny was dismissed. Dr Stacey came in accompanied by Sister, a staff nurse and several junior doctors. His lack of white coat and the expensive suit he wore marked him out from the others. He checked the chart at the end of the bed and then approached Ellen. Tall and slim, it was hard to tell how old he was, perhaps in his forties. His dark hair was threaded with grey at the temples. High cheek-bones and a high-bridged nose gave a hawkish cast to his handsome face. If it were not for his smile, his austere features would have made him look rather severe. He smiled a lot. His teeth were white and even, the dentistry perfect. He was smiling at Sister now, complimenting her on the standard of care. The Sister blushed and twittered her thanks. Ellen could see he was flavour of the month as far as she was concerned. Jenny's doubts were obviously not shared by her superior.

"Hi, Ellen. I'm Dr Frank Stacey. How are you doing?"

The accent was transatlantic with a trace of something else and his smile was now trained on her. Ellen was about to return it when she realized it did not reach his eyes. These were large and dark, browny green, with lighter tints of yellow. Red points showed deep in the irises. Even as she looked the complex patterns seemed to shift and change. Like a kaleidoscope. Ellen acknowledged the accuracy of the description in her great-great-grandmother's diaries, but she would have recognized them anyway – from her own nightmares. She drew the sheet nearer to her and nerved herself to stare back. The eyes filled with cold amusement as he registered her shock.

I know you know, he seemed to say, although not a word passed between them. *And there is nothing, absolutely nothing you can do about it*.

Ellen went through the examination as though in a trance. Her mind was racing, but up and down blind alleys. She was too weak to leave under her own steam, and where could she go? Her family would have her back here in a minute. Maybe she could tell someone, but who? He was her doctor. Tell them what? His last words to his assembled team put an end to that idea. Her only avenue of escape was cut off.

"The signs are pretty good for a full recovery," he said, then his high forehead creased in a frown. "Just one area of concern – she might have sustained some temporary disturbance to the temporal lobes of the brain. What form could this take?"

"Epilepsy?" one of the juniors ventured.

"Hallucination, delusion," another suggested. "Feelings of paranoia."

He nodded. "Certainly possible. I want her monitored very closely. Anything along those lines, I want to know. OK, Ellen?" He turned back to the bed. "Take it easy. I'll see you later. I'm through with you – for now."

Hallucination. Delusion. With a diagnosis like that,

how was anyone ever going to believe her? What was she going to say? *"Hey, excuse me, I've got to get out of here."*

"Oh, why's that?"

"Because my doctor is…"

It sounded like a joke, even to her own ears, let alone anybody else's. Doubts were forming, crowding around her. Perhaps he was right. Perhaps temporal whatsit brain thing was just a posh way of saying "crazy". Like you very well might be if you went round thinking that your doctor was a vampire.

16

"How are you feeling?" Her mother's cheek was cold and smelt of powder and foundation. "You look better, lots better than yesterday. We thought you were…" Her mother's lips pressed together to keep from trembling. "We were so worried – but you seem over the worst now. And you're in good hands. The best, so I understand. Dr Stacey – have you seen him yet?"

Ellen nodded.

"He's very good, apparently. We're lucky—"

"I've seen him before," Ellen interrupted.

"What, dear?"

"Dr Stacey. I've seen him before."

"Last night, you mean? You were barely conscious—"

"No." Ellen shook her head. "I don't mean then. He was outside Gran's house. The first day I was there…"

Her mother frowned. She thought for a moment that Ellen was rambling. They had been warned she might be, well, a bit strange, not quite herself. Then her brow cleared. An odd time to mention it, but it made perfect sense. She'd been talking to him about it only this morning.

"Quite likely. He owns a property quite near Mother's. That's what I want to tell you about…"

"Where is Gran?" Ellen asked. When visiting time came she expected to see her.

"She sends her love, but she's got a bit of a cold. We thought it better if she gives it a few days. Who's this from?" Her mother held up a card, nose wrinkling at the picture on the front. "I call that rather tasteless."

"Let me see. Oh, it's from Andy."

"You mean that boy? The one who kept you out and caused all this? I've had words with Mother about that, I can tell you…"

"I wanted to go. It's not fair to blame her, Mum."

"Well, perhaps not," she replied, the look in her eyes softening. The strain, the tension lines, reminded Ellen again of how much stress her illness put on the family, especially her mother. "Still," she added, "at her age, she should have known better."

"Can he come and see me?"

"Not now, darling. I don't think you quite realize –" Her voice tightened. "Just at the moment it's family visitors only."

"How long will that last?"

"Don't worry yourself about that. You won't be here –"

"How do you mean? Am I going home?"

"Well, not exactly… That's what I wanted to tell you. I'm going to take a look, but I'm sure it's suitable. More than suitable. We've been very lucky. Dr Stacey has agreed to take you. As soon as a bed is available, you are to be transferred to his private clinic."

144

"We can't afford that! It'll cost a fortune!"

"I don't want you to even think about it. We just want the best for you, never mind the money. Dad agrees. We'd find it somehow – but that won't be necessary anyway." Her mother's eyes shone with unshed tears of relief. At last they had found a doctor who could do something. "His initial assessment is very positive and," she took Ellen's hand, and squeezed, "this is the best bit – he has a particular interest in your case. There's some kind of foundation, apparently. Dr Stacey has assured me, it won't cost a penny!"

"What's the matter?"

"Nothing." Ellen turned her head away.

"Yes, there is." Jenny Cheung leaned over to see her better. "What is it?"

Ellen did not answer. She had to pull herself together. She wiped her face on the pillow and sniffed.

"You've got some nice cards," Jenny said, trying to distract her. "Who is this from?" She read the name. "Is he your boyfriend?"

"No," Ellen muttered. "Not really."

"Hasn't he been to see you? Is that why you're upset?"

"Of course not!" Ellen turned back, her tears drying at the thought that she would cry about anything so trivial. "Anyway, Mum says he can't come. Family only."

Jenny put her head to one side. "I could always say I thought he was your brother."

"How is he going to know?"

"I'll get the telephone trolley. You can give him a call."

"Do you know anything about a private clinic run by Dr Stacey?" Ellen asked when the nurse came back.

"Yes." Jenny bent down to plug in the jack. "Some of our patients transfer there for after-care and specialist treatment. Why do you ask?"

"Mum is arranging for me to go there."

"Really? It's very expensive…"

"That doesn't seem to be an issue," Ellen replied. "Is there a problem with it?"

She had detected a level of alarm beneath the surprise in the other girl's voice.

"No," Jenny bit her lip, "it's very good. It's a beautiful place. An old house in its own grounds. More like a hotel than a hospital." She marked the advantages off on her fingers. "Luxury accommodation, not to mention fantastic food and state of the art equipment. A level of care we couldn't even think about providing here."

"But?"

There was something else. Something was not being said.

"I told you. It's very good."

A beeper went off.

"That's for me. I have to go." Jenny's hand went to her belt. She seemed relieved, glad of an excuse to leave. "I'm off duty soon," she added from the door. "So I'll see you tomorrow."

She left Ellen to make her call. She was a nice kid. Jenny liked her enough for what she had just heard to set alarm bells ringing. Her thoughts went to another patient they'd had, a couple of months back. She had also been transferred to Dr Stacey's clinic. Some of the patients he took were very sick, not expected to recover. But others – well. The one she was thinking of had gone from them, seemingly just for convalescence, and within a week she was dead. It happened, of course it did. But how many times? There had been other cases. And there was something else. Staff turnover was high. Someone she knew who worked there had just quit. Jenny had met her the other week. She was vague about her reasons for leaving, just that she'd rather be on the dole than work there again. She wouldn't go back – not if they offered her double, treble, the salary…

17

Ellen woke from a half doze. It was night-time now, everywhere was quiet. She lay wondering what the time was. She found it hard to sleep in hospital. It was always so hot, the plastic covering the mattress made her sweat, and the drip in her arm meant she could not get comfortable. It was never quite dark. Neon strips in the corridor meant light filtered in along the frosted glass top of the partition wall and through her door. All day. All night. Hospital hours stretched to fill the whole twenty-four.

She heard a slight sound, like a foot scraping on the ground, from the farthest corner, near the window. She was aware, quite suddenly, that there was someone in the room with her. She thought at first that it must be Jenny, or one of the others, come by to check on her, but nurses came in and went out. They did not stay, waiting in the shadows, still and unmoving.

"You are awake." Dr Stacey's voice came through the

darkness. He was making a statement, not asking a question.

"You know who I am, don't you." Again, this was not an enquiry.

Ellen nodded. His long legs unfolded. He rose from the chair and he came towards her.

"You are clever. Tell me, Ellen. How do you know so much?"

"I found some diaries…"

"Written by Ellen Laidlaw? Your – what would she be? Great-great-grandmother?"

Ellen nodded again.

"Strange how the past can reach out to us. I have always found that fascinating." He stroked his chin, as though remembering a beard he had once had. "When I knew her I was still the Count Fransz Szekelys. Not yet Dr Frank Stacey. I changed my identity on the stroke of midnight at the beginning of the new century. The world was changing, there was no longer such a place for the aristocracy. I needed another … profession. Dear Anton, Ellen's father, gave me the idea. A doctor was the perfect choice!" His eyes sparked with red lights. "Ninety years and more of death and wars! So much killing. Who would question one or two extra casualties among so many? And who would suspect a doctor? Who would doubt his right to be there, doing what he could, tending the sick, aiding the wounded? For me, it has been a good time. And such advances! I hardly need to feed…"

He reached down and took a unit of blood, popping the seal and drinking like it was a pouch of Ribena.

"It slakes the thirst." He wiped his mouth. Red smeared across the back of his hand. "But it lacks a certain pleasure.

Progress in other fields has suited my purpose also. Take dentistry."

He stretched his lips wide, and removed the smile. The teeth underneath were small and grooved, transparent to the point of discoloration. Sharp-edged, like blades of flint.

"Spoil my looks, don't you think?" His grin widened to disclose long, curving, needle-like canines. "They have even been known to create a certain disquiet. These are the product of genius." He fitted the dentures back into his mouth. "No one would guess what lay beneath. I have several pairs. The man who made them is sadly no longer with us."

"Why me?" It was all she could think of to say. "Aren't there enough people…"

"Do not underestimate yourself, Ellen. You are special." His voice lost its mocking tone and became hard. "The Szekelys have long memories. My cousin died. There is a blood price. I myself was nearly destroyed. It took a long time for me to recover from the actions of your kinswoman."

"Why should I have to pay for what she did?"

"That would be enough. But perhaps you are not so clever after all. You obviously don't fully comprehend your part in this. Let me explain. When I say that you are special, I do not use the term idly. You carry something like a gene, akin to my own, through Ellen's mother, Isobella. It is recessive, not every person carries it. This accounts for your present illness. I am an expert. In blood, naturally. I am well known in the field. In difficult cases, I am consulted. Yours is a difficult case." He shrugged. "Your doctors come to me for help…"

"Naturally." Ellen echoed his word, bitter despair creeping into her voice.

He laughed, a thin, hollow sound, as though she had said something witty.

"Don't fight, Ellen. There is no point. There is no cure for your condition. Without me you will die. Wasting away, day after day, until in a month, maybe two…" He blew on the palm of his hand, as if her life had become impossibly light, to be dispersed with a breath, like thistledown. "I am your only hope."

To become a vampire? That was a choice? Why didn't he do it now? Why didn't he get started?

He seemed to read her thoughts.

"How do you know I have not?" he said.

She looked down at her arm. The tapes securing the IV drip were loose, like they had been undone, then reapplied.

"You still don't understand. You are not just an ordinary –" he searched for the right word – "subject. Some are like this –" he crumpled the empty plastic pouch – "a quick fix and that is it. What I have in mind for you is quite different. This place is too public. Initiation takes time. And privacy. It is being arranged."

This was mad. Crazy. She must be hallucinating. This could not be happening. Ellen closed her eyes, trying to shut him out. When she opened them again, he had gone. Perhaps he had never been there at all. She rolled over, trying to find a more comfortable sleeping position. He was real all right. By the side of her bed, uncurling on the floor, lay a discarded blood pouch.

18

"Goodness! How did that get there?" The nurse who came to her in the morning was a stranger. "It must have fallen out of the waste." She pounced on the empty plastic pouch. "Honestly! Some of these auxiliaries are so careless! Sister would have an absolute fit!"

"Where's Jenny?" Ellen asked.

"She'll be on again later. Let me dispose of this first and then we'll get you tidied. Rounds will be starting in a minute."

Which meant he would be back at her bedside again. Ellen stared at the wall, sick at the very thought of seeing him. After last night, never would be soon enough.

Ellen worried needlessly, Dr Stacey was not in the hospital that morning. She got the registrar instead. Tired and harassed, he carried out his examination as quickly as possible, rapped out orders to Sister, and swept on to the next patient.

She saw no one after that. She counted the hours, minutes even, to visiting time. Andy had promised to be there, but Ellen could find a thousand possible delays, and a thousand more perfectly good reasons for him not to be able to make it. She had to see him. She would tell him about Dr Stacey and last night's visitation. He would listen. And he would believe her. He had to. He was her only hope.

"Hi." Andy came through the door, jiffy bag under one arm, bunch of flowers under the other.

"Hi."

"How are you?"

"All right. Andy, come here. We don't have much time and I've got to talk to you. Have you read the diaries?"

"Yeah. Your gran gave them to me. I brought them with me. Thought maybe you'd want them by you." He put them in her bedside cabinet. "Like you said, they make weird reading."

"It gets weirder."

"How do you mean?"

"What if I told you I'd seen the Count."

"You've seen him!" Andy's own eyes grew wide. He stared at her for a moment in silent astonishment, then lines of doubt crossed his forehead. "But I don't see how you could." He shook his head. "That's not possible. If he's in the diaries, how can he be around now?"

"He is! I'm telling you! He's here – in the hospital! And I've seen him before…".

"Where?"

"He was standing in the street opposite Gran's—"

"Hey! Wait! Wait a minute…" Andy frowned again as

he recalled the stranger he had bumped into after he left Ellen's house. "What does he look like? Tall. Funny eyes. Odd accent. Kind of transatlantic?"

Ellen nodded.

"Yes. How do you know?"

"I saw him myself, outside the house. How do you know it's Szekelys?"

"I recognized him, from the diaries and – and –" this was going to be hard – "I've been having dreams in which he appeared. And last night, he came to my room. He calls himself Stacey now." Despite trying not to, Ellen felt herself beginning to break down. "Andy, I'm so scared!"

"But even if he is…" Andy gestured to the walls, the bustle of the wards, noise in the corridors. "Even if he's the same person, what can he do in here?"

"A lot." Ellen tightened her grip on him. "He's my doctor!"

Andy could think of no reply. He put his arm round her.

There was a knock. A nurse appeared round the door.

"Hi, Ellen. Oh, you must be Andy. I'm Jenny. Jenny Cheung."

"Pleased to meet you."

The nurse smiled. "I hate to break you up," she said to Ellen, "but your mother is on her way. I'll pop in when she's gone. Catch you later."

"She seems all right."

"Yes," Ellen replied, wiping her eyes, "she's very nice. Andy –"

"It's OK. Look. Try not to worry… I'll be back tomorrow."

"Ah, Mrs Forrest." Jenny's voice came extra loud

154

through the partition. "Sister would like a word – in her office. It's this way…"

Andy leaned over and kissed her swiftly.

"I'll think of something."

Andy walked along the corridor thinking about Ellen. He seemed to spend a lot of time doing that and yet, a week or so ago, she had hardly been in his mind at all. A kid he used to play with. A face he could hardly recall. Now it was different. He never stopped thinking about her, but what good was that to Ellen? She was desperately ill. Very sick. But that was physical. This other thing was at the root of her current problem, making her so upset. What she told him, about this doctor being Szekelys, was it possible?

"Paging Dr Stacey, Dr Stacey."

The man walking towards him stopped in his tracks and looked round, searching for a phone. Recognition came even before Andy registered the name. It was the guy he'd seen the other night, the one who'd been hanging around outside Ellen's house. The one with the disappearing footsteps. Andy stopped by a Coke machine and pretended to select from the drinks display.

The guy picked a receiver off the wall and said into it, "Stacey here."

He spoke for a moment or two, and then replaced the handset. He looked over at Andy and their eyes met. Unable to break the gaze, unable to turn away from the derisive smile on Stacey's face, Andy stared into eyes which seemed to mirror his inmost doubts.

You'll think of something – like what? they mocked. *So what if it's true? What are you going to do about it?*

155

19

Ellen tried not to sleep. She tried very hard to stay awake, to stay conscious, to be aware of every little thing, every little movement; but she must have dropped off because suddenly she knew he was there in the room with her.

"So," his voice came from the same shadowy corner, "it is all decided. Did your mother tell you?"

Ellen did not reply. She could see him now, the outline of his body, sitting, legs crossed, one knee over the other, long white fingers steepled beneath his chin.

"You will find it very comfortable –" A long thin hand indicated the room. "Much better than here. It was a hospital before, of course, but for the mentally sick. We have transformed it. Now it is as luxurious as any hotel. You will like it," he was standing now, walking towards her, "the grounds especially. We have our own private chapel. Many patients and their families find it a place of peace, a place of comfort. Some of my patients are, alas, terminal cases and their parents often request that they are laid to rest there. It is so beautiful, so tranquil, the churchyard is so well kept, that even after death," he smiled, revealing his sharp inner teeth, "they feel their loved ones are being looked after. You will not lack for company."

His eyes sought hers and held them. Ellen tried to look away and could not. She stared, eyes wide, unable even to blink, she could not move a muscle.

His gaze shifted to her throat. He reached down, brushing her hair back from her neck, searching for her pulse. Ellen could feel the blood slowly beating against fingers so cold their touch burned her skin. She watched as his cheeks became rigid and his lips began to retract. Then, as a cat might sheathe its claws, he drew back.

"Dr Stacey. We weren't expecting you on the ward tonight. Is everything all right?" Jenny Cheung's question, although polite, was edged with suspicion.

"Yes, thank you, Nurse. Everything's fine." His voice had lost its ice and oozed easy charm. "I was just checking on our patient here. That's all. Good-night."

"Good-night, Doctor."

Jenny did not trust him. She went over to the bed to check Ellen herself. One glance was enough to tell her something was badly wrong. She'd seen this kind of shock before. It was not physical, more a kind of psychological shutting off; like when someone had received some stunning news which laid waste to their emotions, devastating them utterly. It happened when you had to tell a patient, or their parents, however gently, that their case was hopeless, there was little chance of recovery.

"What did he say to you?" she asked, but got no answer.

Jenny reviewed the options. A tranquillizer would calm her, but it would only treat the symptoms, it could not get to the deeper cause of the girl's distress. Perhaps she should call in an expert. They had some excellent counsellors, skilled in this kind of thing. Maybe something to quiet her now and bring someone in to talk to her in the morning. Jenny had just decided on that course of action, when Ellen spoke.

"Do you believe in vampires?" she said.

20

Jenny agreed to stay through the rest of the night. The presence of the nurse meant no more visits, and no more dreams, no nightmares. Ellen slept well and woke refreshed with a plan ready formed, clear in her head. All it needed was Jenny's agreement, which she gave, without reservation.

What choice did she have? Ellen was a patient in her care. She could not stand by and see her abused, physically or mentally, by anybody, whoever he was. And she couldn't report him. For what? Checking on one of his patients? It was her word against his. Stacey was a senior consultant; compared with him, Jenny was nobody. Anyway, he had the girl covered. Any hint of what she'd told Jenny and he'd say she was paranoid, psychotic. If they were going to get him, they'd have to find another way and Ellen's plan was as good as any.

Off duty now, Jenny boarded a bus and found a seat. The girl was clearly very frightened, but Jenny did not take that as a sign of temporal lobe disturbance. She had her own reasons for accepting her story.

The first one was to do with Dr Stacey. She distrusted him, and this had nothing to do with Ellen. She had never felt comfortable with him, sensing someone else lay behind that suave manner and sharky smile. He was the one who had warned them that Ellen might seem disturbed, that her word was not to be believed.

The second reason was Ruth, the friend who had gone to work for him. Ruth was a down-to-earth Geordie, a cheerful, practical, utterly no-nonsense type of person. They had worked together, they had been friends, then Ruth decided to leave the hospital. Jenny did not blame her for going for the better money and easier working conditions to be found in the private sector, but they had not seen much of each other after that. They had met up a week or so ago, purely by chance.

Jenny had suggested a coffee, a chat about old times — this was when she found out that Ruth was no longer at Stacey's clinic, Cedar Lodge. She had been strangely reluctant to explain her reasons for leaving, not too keen on talking about it at all, but it was soon clear that she was not going back there, not ever, wild horses wouldn't drag her. Curious, Jenny had wanted to know more.

Ruth's good-natured, rounded face had suddenly taken on a drawn, haunted look, and her soft brown eyes had cast anxiously around the coffee shop, as though she feared they might be overheard. Wrapping her hands round the comforting warmth of her mug, she had muttered into it about "Strange things going on down there – unbelievable, really". Inexplicable relapses, deaths not expected, incidents hard to explain in any rational way. A "weird carry-on altogether", she had called it. She seemed nervous, frightened even, and Jenny didn't pressure her further. Their conversation moved on to easier, safer topics. They had parted soon after that, and Jenny had not seen her since, but she had formed the distinct impression that there was something very wrong about Stacey's set-up – and this was long before she ever encountered Ellen Forrest.

The third reason was the diaries. The jiffy bag had been sealed when Ellen handed it over. As the girl slept, Jenny had read the contents.

It was all there. The third volume started with an account of following the Count through the night-time East End streets. The abduction, the part on board ship with the Count and the Countess, it had all happened just as Ellen had described it.

Ellen's near drowning had brought on pneumonia. At some time she must have asked Tom to write his own account, which he had done. It was slotted in at the back. A single sheet in neat spiky writing, quite different from Ellen's hand.

Undated, it started:

My Dearest Ellen,

You have asked me to write my version of events on that terrible night. Here is my account.

As soon as I found you were gone, I knew he had taken you. Fearing for your life, for your soul, I went in search of Caspar. He was at Hudson's Wharf, down by the river. He and his friends had been monitoring the port of London. They had discovered a schooner, bound for a port in the Black Sea, chartered to Szekelys. The captain was vague about the date for sailing, but much had been loaded, the ship was being made ready. Caspar was keeping watch on it. When I got there he told me the Count and Countess had not yet boarded. I greeted the news with intense relief, for I feared the boat might have already sailed with you in it, but they would have to wait until the full of the tide, Caspar said. The only time that vampires can cross running water is with the flood.

A sudden mist, a sea fret, came creeping up as the river filled, obscuring the black schooner. Across the water, we could hear the creak of the gang plank and the cursing of the seamen as they loaded what we glimpsed as a heavy casket. We heard the Count greet the captain and the Countess's deep throaty laugh. As the ship manoeuvred out into deeper water, we followed in a small dinghy. We rowed as near as we dared and were preparing to board her, when we heard the cry, "Fire!" We saw Ivan approach the rail and drop something over the side. Thank God you fell near to us. Your skirts buoyed you for a moment before you sank, Caspar noted the place and dived in. When he brought you to the surface, I feared you had drowned, but we found a pulse, faint and fluttering. Caspar and I worked to revive you. When you began to breathe again, I confess I thought we had witnessed a miracle.

I went straight to your father and told him all that had occurred. He was almost beside himself with anxiety about you, and anger at his own blindness to the true nature of the Count and Countess and his pride which insisted that the Count's condition was purely medical and that he could cure it. I also opened my heart to him

and told him of my love for you. I had nearly lost you. I couldn't help myself. I did not even know then if my feeling was reciprocated. I know now, and I cannot tell you how happy that has made me.
Your loving,
Tom

There was a postscript:

Ivan appeared back at the Hospital and, when I told Doctor Laidlaw the part he had played in your rescue, he welcomed him gladly. The captain and crew of the schooner escaped the conflagration, but of the Count and Countess, no trace was ever found. Nothing is known...

Until now. The bus jolted, as it approached the stop, bringing Jenny back to the present. Andy was sitting on the wall, waiting for her.

He didn't know her at first. She looked different in ordinary clothes, suede jacket, jeans and boots. Her black hair was immaculately cut into a short bob. He thought she was a student.

"Hi." He scrambled down from his perch. "Sorry, I—"

She smiled. "Didn't recognize me? That's OK, hardly anybody does when out of uniform. Thanks for coming, Andy."

"Ellen? How is she?"

"She's much better – physically. Her blood count is up and she no longer needs the IV drips. But..."

"But what?"

Jenny told him about the visit from Stacey.

"I've also read the diaries," she added. "Last night,

while she slept. Ellen's come up with a plan and I've agreed to help her."

"What is it?"

"It is very simple. Tonight, before Stacey comes to call, we swap places."

Andy stared at her. "How's that going to work? She's … and you're…"

"Chinese? Half Chinese," Jenny corrected. "We are similar in height and build. The hospital has a beauty service – so patients can look their best, they think it's therapeutic—"

"So?"

"I've booked Ellen a hair cut for ten o'clock this morning. Before Stacey does his rounds, so he can see it – then later he won't think it odd. If we change places," Jenny went on, "it means she's safe. I'm going to use this." She took a voice-activated Dictaphone out of her pocket. "So if he tries something we'll have it all recorded."

"But – if he *is* a vampire – that's not going to stop him. You can't take her place every night for the rest of your life."

"I know." Jenny had taken Ellen's plan and put her own spin on it. "That's what I'm going to see about now. I want you to come with me."

"Where are we going?"

"Chinatown. We have our own vampires. Chinese vampires," Jenny told him as they walked along the crowded streets, "called *Kang-shi*. They are the spirits of dead people. Animated by blood, just like European ones. They have blazing red eyes and wear ancient costume of, I don't know, I think Ming dynasty. They move in groups of maybe four, holding their arms like this." She extended her arms full length and demonstrated. "They jump wherever they go."

"Tend to stand out in a crowd, then?"

Andy cast up and down the road, surveying the pre-Christmas shoppers, pretending to be on the lookout for a troupe of hopping Chinese vampires.

Jenny laughed. "They have become a bit of a joke, and there have been some terrible movies. I guess nobody believes in them now, not really, but they are evil. Malevolent."

"How do you get rid of them?"

"In the usual way. Wooden stake and –" She ended with the downward chopping movement of the hands. "But there are other methods."

21

Andy couldn't read the sign but the letters on the door said "Centre for Chinese Herbal Medicine". The stand in the window held glass bottles containing the kind of dried herbs and spices you might find in a health food shop, but a second glance confirmed that the fibrous, hairy pieces of bark and the strangely twisted roots were from plants he had never seen before. The jars sat next to miniature feet and porcelain heads, all marked out into sections. Behind them was an anatomical chart, but it looked different from the ones Andy remembered from school. The body, flayed to the muscle, was etched with lines. Energy channels, Jenny called them, meridians. It had something to do with acupuncture.

They had come here to see Jenny's uncle. This was his shop. She spoke to the young man on reception and then left with him. Andy had no idea what she had said, they conversed in Chinese. He had plenty of time to study the chart before she came back.

"My uncle will see us now," she said.

Andy followed her into a consulting room. He did not know what to expect, but there was a computer on the desk and the man who came to greet them was wearing a silver-grey suit and looked like a businessman. It was hard to tell his age. He was slim and spare with smooth skin and silvering hair. Andy would have placed him at maybe fifty or so, but when he smiled, his face broke up into a million lines. His small dark eyes were shrewd and wise, his gaze unwavering and steady.

He listened carefully, nodding now and again, as Jenny spoke to him in rapid Chinese. When he eventually replied it was in English, formal, correct and slightly accented.

"What you request," he said, "is most unusual. Not to say unorthodox. My instinct tells me to say I cannot help you. I'm a respectable practitioner, not a witch doctor –" he held up a hand to stem any interruption – "but as you are my niece, and I owe your father certain favours – I'll see what I can do. There is a potion effective against *Kang-shi*." He looked over at Andy. "Whether it will work upon your European variety –" he spread his small well-manicured hands – "that is another matter."

"It's our only chance," Andy said.

"Then you will have to take it. But make no mistake. You might not be able to act twice. The potion works as a poison. It might take effect quickly, in which case you will be rid of the problem, or it might be slow. In that case you will have to go after him, find him."

"Where will he go?"

"His home earth. A coffin. A vault. From what you tell me, he can normally exist without resorting to this place

167

every day, but it will exist, and if he is poisoned, weakened, he would have to return to it to recover. You would have to seek him out and dispatch him. Quickly. Within a day. I can give you things to trap him."

"Like what?" Andy asked.

"Papers. Spells, I suppose you would call them, and threads soaked in the potion. They will keep him inert until you are ready to act. Remember, he has great strength, more than several full-grown men put together, and driving a stake through the heart is not as easy as it looks in the movies." His manner became businesslike again. "It will take me time to assemble the ingredients. I have some of them here but by no means all. Some are rare, difficult to get hold of, and I will have to consult practitioners in other arts, not just medicine."

"How long?" Jenny asked.

"Tonight."

"What time?"

"I can't say for sure. Call me."

"Thank you." Jenny bowed to him.

He frowned, suddenly looking his years. "Don't thank me yet," he said and reached for the phone.

They left her uncle and went to a café in Soho.

"Even if you get the stuff," Andy said, when the coffee came, "I still don't see how you're going to get Stacey to take it."

"I'm going to drink it," Jenny replied. "So if he is a vampire, he'll take it in, won't he?"

"Oh, hey, I don't know…" Andy frowned. "That sounds really risky."

"Well? What do you propose?"

He shrugged and stirred his coffee.

"Exactly. It's the only way, Andy. Believe me…"

"I'm not saying that, but –"

"Can you think of anything else?"

"Well, no. Not right now…"

"There you are, then. I don't think we have any choice. Anyway, it might not come to that…"

They both knew it would. She looked at him and their eyes met.

"I'm a big girl. I can handle it. Don't worry about me. Now, you go and see Ellen."

Andy walked to the hospital. They had decided not to tell Ellen about the Chinese vampire remedy. She would never agree to Jenny taking such a risk for her sake. If she knew about that she might not go ahead with the swap at all. It was best not to worry her. What she didn't know couldn't hurt her.

Ellen's room was second on the right before the main ward. The door was closed. Andy knocked gently but there was no reply. He knocked again, this time more loudly, and immediately felt guilty. He wanted to see her, talk to her, but if she was asleep, it was wrong to wake her. He put his ear to the door and listened. Still nothing. He pushed the handle, meaning just to peep in. If she was sleeping he would call back later.

The door swung open wide. Andy felt his heart lurch up and lodge in his throat. The bed was stripped. Bedding neatly stacked. All the equipment gone, leaving a panel of empty sockets. Andy stood and stared, as though the room itself could offer an explanation, and then he relaxed. He must have taken a wrong turning. That was it. Easy enough to do. After all, everything appeared the same along these miles and miles of corridors. He looked at the name. It was the right ward.

Either that, or they've moved her. They were always shifting people about.

Either that, or...

A hospital bed, stripped and empty. There was only one other explanation.

Just then the Staff Nurse walked past. She read his stricken face and smiled.

"Hey! It's OK! She's moved, that's all."

"Where to? Another part of the hospital?" Andy glanced towards the long connecting corridor.

"No. She's gone to Cedar Lodge. Do you know it?"

Andy nodded. He knew it all right. It was not far from where he lived. A big place, ex-NHS, it had been empty for quite a time. He had seen the work going on, seen the notices – "acquired for private development" – but had no idea who owned it now. The grounds were extensive and, on one side at least, bordered on to the cemetery.

"A bed became available. She was moved this afternoon," the nurse went on, taking his silence as a request for more information. "Dr Stacey can take better care of her there. It's his private clinic."

It seemed to Jenny that she had only just closed her eyes, only just put her head on the pillow, when the phone began to ring.

"Who is it?"

"It's me, Andy. Sorry to disturb you," he added, "but it's Ellen. I went to the hospital…"

"What's happened?" Jenny was wide awake now.

"They've moved her – to Stacey's place. I've tried phoning, but they won't tell me anything. They won't even say how she is, let alone let me speak to her. Now he's got her there – anything we planned, I don't see how it can work…" She could hear the frustration in his voice breaking towards panic. "What are we going to do?"

"Where are you?"

"I'm still at the hospital."

"OK. Meet me at my uncle's."

"When?"

"Half an hour."

Jenny put the phone down and checked the clock. Five-fifteen. A quick call to her uncle told her that the remedy would be ready about six. She punched in the numbers for another call.

"Hello, Ruth Perry speaking…"

"Hi, Ruth. This is Jenny. Jenny Cheung."

Ruth sounded friendly, glad to hear from her. Jenny smiled and explained what she wanted. She believed in luck, and so far hers was holding. Which was good. Somehow she had the feeling that, before the night was out, she was going to need as much of it as she could get.

"Have you got it?" Andy asked as she came out of the shop. Jenny showed him the porcelain bottle. It was white with an almost translucent blue tinge. About four inches high, narrow at the neck and broad at the base. It was stoppered, sealed with red wax, and tied with black silk threads.

"What's in it?"

"Don't ask. I'm serious!" She frowned at his grin and fingered the flattened seal, reading like braille the imprinted characters. "Some things it is better not to know."

22

"I'll be with you in a minute. Perhaps you would like to take a seat?"

The young woman at the reception desk smiled from behind the telephone. The Cedar Lodge name tag read *Cathy Pierce*.

Andy smiled back but remained standing at the counter. He looked round. The foyer was impressive: deeply carpeted, soft music playing, comfortable furniture grouped around glass coffee tables strewn with glossy magazines. It looked more like an expensive country hotel, or health club, than a hospital.

"Now." The young woman had finished her telephone call. "What can I do for you?"

"Well, Cathy, I'm enquiring about my sister..."

The heavy glass doors were pushed open behind him, and a figure, wrapped up against the freezing conditions, came over to the counter. The stevedore's hat, pulled well down, stayed in place, but a gloved hand moved the muffling scarf before she spoke.

"Hi. I'm Su Lin Chen. The agency sent me."

The young woman behind the desk frowned and checked her schedules.

"I don't appear to have a note of it…"

"Someone phoned this afternoon. A couple of people off with flu, or something."

"I'm just dealing with this query, if you'll just hang on a minute. Now, sir. What is your sister's name?"

"Ellen. Ellen Forrest."

"And when was she admitted?"

"This afternoon, I believe."

"Here it is. Ellen Forrest. Bluebell Ward. Room 12. That's ground floor. East Wing."

"Can't I go through?" the agency nurse interrupted. "I'm late as it is."

"Do you know where to go?"

"I've worked here before."

Front desk was supposed to be informed of any additions to staffing but she was here now and, even if she went away, the agency could still bill the clinic.

"Go on, then. Report to the nursing officer."

Cathy waved her towards the second corridor.

"I'm sorry about that. Now, where were we?"

Andy leaned over the counter, nice and friendly, and began a lengthy spiel, a whole family history, so the receptionist's attention was elsewhere and she did not notice the agency nurse walk straight past the door which led to the Chief Nursing Officer and take the one that read Bluebell Ward.

"So, you see, I'd really like to see her," Andy went on. "I've come a long way. Down from Newcastle – I'm studying up there. I came as soon as I heard she had been taken so ill, but when I got to the hospital they told me she'd been transferred…"

Cathy listened patiently, while he talked on, knowing that, however poignant and moving his story, the answer was still going to be "no". Visiting time finished ages ago. Visitors were welcome in the day, but in the evening they were forbidden, unless by prior arrangement. Dr Stacey was strict about this, she explained. Some of their patients were very sick. They needed rest. Visitors could be very taxing, and anyway, there were systems. There had been problems in the past with patients' families demanding access at all hours of the day and night. Make an exception for one and the place would be overrun. He would have to come back tomorrow.

"Hey – I've got to go back north tomorrow! Just this once, can't you make an exception?"

Cathy sighed, ready to go through all the reasons again. The agency nurse walked past, muffled up to go out, suede coat collar turned, anticipating the cold. She can't have been needed after all. The agency's fault, no doubt. A mix-up with the dates. They were always doing that.

"OK, OK," Andy said, holding up his hands, signifying defeat. "You win. I'll stay over. See you."

He grinned and waved as he got to the door. Cold came in as he followed the nurse out. He had given in quicker than Cathy expected.

Outside, Ellen took off the hat and shook out her hair. It was cut short, like Jenny's.

"Are you all right?" Andy put his arm round her. "Sure you are strong enough?"

"I feel better for getting out of there." Ellen unwound

the scarf and smiled. "Anyway, I'll have to be, won't I?"

"Come on, then. I borrowed my brother's car. We'll go to his place. It's not far from here. Did it go OK, with Jenny?"

"Yes. Fine."

It had been like the answer to a prayer, seeing Jenny coming through the door. Ellen said she didn't have to do it, not now. But Jenny insisted. Told her not to worry, it was all sorted. She'd do it and then get out. She'd got hold of a uniform. She could leave with the other nurses.

"I'm going to be here, to meet her. That's if it goes OK…"

"If what goes OK?" Alerted by his uncertainty, Ellen looked up at him. "There's something else, isn't there?"

"Yes."

"Tell me."

"It's better if you don't know…"

"Tell me!"

Andy explained about the Chinese remedy.

"How is she going to administer it?" Ellen asked, but she didn't need to, she suddenly knew. Jenny was going to use her own blood like a serum to get into his system.

"Oh, Andy, no!" She turned back towards the clinic, horrified. "It should be me! That's not right!"

Andy pulled her back.

"It's too dangerous. It might poison you. Anyway, it's too late, she will have taken it by now. Leave it." Andy held her tight. "Leave it!"

It was the dead time of night, when sleep is deep and dreamless and even those who work through the hours until morning, shift workers, nurses on duty, feel their eyelids grow heavy and jerk to wakefulness only to find themselves drowsing again.

Cedar Lodge was in the grip of a quiet so absolute, so all-pervasive, that even the slightest noise was exaggerated; but he made no sound as he went down the bottom corridor towards Ellen's room. He cast no shadow in the blue half-tones of the emergency lighting. Neither did his image show as he passed reflective surfaces: paintings and picture glass, mirrors on the walls, frosted glass doorways. Over years, over centuries, he had perfected the ability to slip from one state to another easily. By day or night he could pass as human, as Dr Stacey, if he chose to, if it was in his interest to do so; but this night was different, this night he was other, he was the Count Fransz Szekelys.

This night was special, although few in modern Britain would know it. Perhaps in Catholic countries where saints' days are acknowledged, perhaps there people would know that tomorrow, 30th November, was St Andrew's Day. In his own country it would be different. Across a continent ribboned with autobahns, scanned by satellites, dotted with vast industrial conurbations, nuclear power stations, petrochemical complexes, there were still people, his people, deep in the country or high in the mountains, who would remember it was the Eve of St Andrew.

They would know to be home before the sun went down, would know that, at the stroke of midnight, all things evil were loosed and free to walk the earth. In countries where such beliefs, or any beliefs, had been outlawed for fifty years or more, old women would cross themselves and see to their households, securing doors and windows with more than locks and catches: wreaths of garlic, crosses of ash, thorns of the wild rose, branch of the rowan, sprigs of holly. In societies renowned for their kindness, for their hospitality, on this night no stranger would be welcome, no one would be invited across the threshold lest they be undead, revenant – *obour, strigoi, vrykolakas, vampyr, nosferatu.*

He reached the last room. It was the only one occupied on this corner of the building. The one next to it, the one above, and those across the corridor, had recently been vacated. He paused, savouring the moment, then bony fingers reached down. Long nails, pointed like claws, skittered on the paintwork as he slowly turned the handle of the door.

He entered with his senses heightened. Individual grains of pollen, each one distinct, scattered on the table, clung to the roughened top surface of outward curling petals, fleshy and veined like human tongues. A clock chimed, miles away, deep in the city; in the corner, the delicate hum of a spider spinning its web.

This detailed definition went as he approached the bed. The need to feed was so strong that his eyes filmed with a thick crimson glaze. He saw as if through red gauze. The room, and everything in it, shades of scarlet. The only sound he heard now was the roaring beat, strong and regular, of human arterial blood.

She lay with her face away from him. Her hair, cut short the day before, exposed the long neck. He bent towards her, choosing a spot about an inch below the ear. He bit once, tenderly, playfully, before slicing down with his razor-sharp incisors. Her eyes rolled up under the eyelids. He had all the time in the world. He could stay here until daybreak, if he chose to, and she would not wake, would not stir, would never even know.

23

The shift at the clinic changed before dawn. Andy and Ellen were back in the car park waiting as the staff began to drift out. One or two stood chatting but most hurried off, anxious to get home, tired after a long night.

Jenny appeared, still in her uniform, hands in her cardigan pockets. She came straight to the car and got in the back seat.

"Are you all right?" Ellen asked.

Jenny nodded. She looked very pale.

"So? What happened?" Andy turned to her. "Did Stacey come?"

"Yes. Well, I don't know for sure it was him," her hand went to her neck, "but something did."

"What's that?"

The right side of her neck was covered in a square gauze pad.

"A dressing. I got it from the nurses' station."

Jenny carefully undid the tapes. Andy expected to see

two neat punctures, like in the movies, but it was more of a gash, a deep slit, starting an inch under the ear and extending down the neck about a finger's length. It was not red, or swollen, but looked ugly, puckered, like a wound that has been in water. The edges, slightly turned out, were pale and bluish.

"Does it hurt?" Ellen asked.

Jenny shook her head. "No, it doesn't. That's the odd thing. It doesn't hurt a bit. I'll be fine," she managed a weak smile, "don't worry."

Relieved, Ellen got out of the car.

Andy turned from the driver's seat.

"Ellen! What are you doing?"

"I've got to go back, Andy, before they miss me. If I go in now – with the day shift – I won't look so conspicuous. I *have to* – don't try and argue. If they can't find me, there will be a massive fuss…"

"I suppose so…"

He could see the logic, but after what had happened to Jenny he was reluctant to let her out of his sight.

"OK. But don't take any risks, Ellen. You've got to promise…"

"I promise. I'm out of there today – as soon as it can be arranged. And if it can't – I'll discharge myself."

"Where is Stacey now?" Andy asked as he watched Ellen make her way through the doors. "Is he still in the building?"

Jenny shrugged. "I don't know, he might be. Inside, there's a duty board. His name's still on it."

"His car hasn't moved."

His Jaguar was parked under a sign with his name on it.

"There he goes!"

Jenny grabbed Andy's arm and pointed to a dark figure slipping out of a side door. He ignored his car, went straight past it, and carried on round the edge of the building, keeping close to the wall.

Andy opened his door.

"Where are you going?"

"After him. Give me that bag."

Jenny picked it up from the seat beside her. The rucksack seemed nearly empty but it weighed heavy. She knew what was inside it.

"Take this…" she started to say and then she remembered. The stuff her uncle had given her was with Ellen, in the pocket of her coat.

"It's all right." Andy had raided his brother's tool shed, helping himself to a cold chisel and mallet, as well as a heavy duty torch and a couple of batteries. "I've got what I need right here."

"Good luck. Be careful!"

"Thanks. I will." He slung the bag on to his shoulder. "See you later."

Andy went off across the car park towards the rear of the building. He did not have to say where he was going. The grounds spread down from the back of the clinic to a long stone wall which marked the northern boundary of the cemetery.

He was soon out of sight, swallowed by morning mist. With the approaching day it seemed to thicken, as it sometimes does at this time of year, prolonging the hours of darkness, making dawn seem a long time coming.

Jenny woke from a light doze, roused by a tapping next to her head.

182

"Hi, I didn't mean to startle you," Ellen said as Jenny wound down the window. "I brought you these." She handed over a plastic bag containing the clothes from last night. "Mum brought mine in this morning." The clinic was not like the hospital. Patients did not have to sit about in pyjamas. If they could possibly manage it, they were encouraged to get up and move about. "I came out as soon as I could. Where's Andy?"

"He's gone after Stacey. Down into the cemetery, I guess. He hasn't come back yet."

"When did he leave?"

"Before daybreak. Just after you."

They looked at each other. That was hours ago. What if he was lost in there? What if there had been an accident? The place contained other dangers, apart from Stacey. In some parts, huge holes gaped under thin layers of disguising vegetation. In others, a single skin of crumbling brick was all that lay between the world above and vast underground vaults, labyrinths of passages.

"Maybe we ought to go after him," Ellen said, breaking the silence between them.

"I'll go."

Jenny emptied the bag of clothes.

"Not on your own." Ellen shook her head. "We both go."

"How do you feel?" Jenny asked, struggling into her jeans. "Will you be strong enough?"

"I feel fine," Ellen replied.

Certainly, the girl looked better than Jenny had ever seen her. Her eyes shone. Her colour was good. The poison must be working its way through Stacey's veins. Her uncle had told her: as the girl grows strong, he grows weaker.

"Won't you be missed?"

"This is more important. Anyway, I'm leaving later. They can put it down as an early departure. Come on. We've got to find Andy."

Jenny checked her coat. The stuff was still in her pocket. If Andy hadn't done it already, they had to get to Stacey and destroy him. If they did not, Ellen would grow weak again. And she herself, she put her hand to her neck, she would also be affected.

"Right. Let's go."

She got out of the car, slamming the door. More talk would waste time. They had until sundown.

24

The cemetery was vast. It sprawled away from them, down the hillside, covering acres of ground.

The fog, which had seemed to clear, lingered here. Water dripped off dark evergreen trees and branches bare of leaves. Only the holly showed any kind of colour. No wonder it was supposed to be a tree which brought good luck and kept away evil spirits.

It was quiet. No sound penetrated from outside, not even a siren or the hum of traffic. Only bird cries and the scurrying of animals disturbed the silence.

Ellen squinted, trying to see through the trees, quartering the whole area, searching for Andy. Funereal shrubs, like yew and box, had grown to twenty, thirty feet. Self-seeded saplings were now forest high. Brambles rampaged everywhere, swamping the stone monuments. Blackened by time, greened by slime, tombs showed as just lumps, humps in a sea of ivy. Square chambers had collapsed in on themselves, vandalized, destroyed by neglect and time, huge stone slabs cast aside, cracked open wide to expose black interiors. Stone angels, massive wings chipped or missing, rose to gaze blindly, snapped fingers pointing up at the sky.

"Down there!" Jenny's sharp eyes had picked it out. Far below them, right over the other side, a flash of blue and white.

"Could be."

Andy was wearing an anorak with an Adidas stripe.

The path, such as it was, led in a broad curve to the right. The sides were eroded, stone slabs had cracked and lifted, gravel had disappeared under a thick quilting of moss. It led downwards in a long, tightening spiral. Soon the place where they started from was far above them, no longer in sight.

Up ahead there was a big sunken circle. A huge cedar brooded over the whole area, its boughs spread through the thinning mist like dark strata. It was not a place to linger. They walked past wide cloistered arches, behind which lay crumbling catacombs. Some of these had been broken into, their mouldering contents spilled on the ground. Ragged holes gaped where the stone had been smashed. Strange symbols defaced the pillars. This was not casual vandalism, or the work of children. At the centre of the circular pavement lay small heaps of wood, charred and blackened, the remains of fires.

They stayed out in the open, keeping as far as possible from the perimeter. They were at the dark heart of the Victorian part of the cemetery. Discounting the way they had entered, three pathways led out. These were lined by large structures, some free standing, others half set into the hillside. They lay above ground, some as big as houses, with porticoed entrances: all were blind and windowless. In life, the families lodged in these vaults and mausoleums had enjoyed wealth and importance. Their last dwelling places were built to reflect this, to make sure death brought with it no embarrassing drop in status.

Ellen turned slowly, gazing from one path to another. Which direction? Which route had he taken?

"Any ideas?"

Andy came up behind her. His hand on her shoulder made her jump a mile.

She turned to face him. His jacket and trousers were ripped and muddied all down one side. Dried blood beaded on scratches raked across his cheek and forehead.

"It's nothing." He put a hand to his face. His nails were blackened and broken, the skin torn by vicious thorns. "I, er, tried for a short cut and took a tumble, that's all. It was a while before I could climb out."

"Did you see where he went?"

Andy shrugged. "How do you follow a mist within a mist? When I got in here, it was still dark, and very foggy. I had him in my sights, but then he seemed to sink and disappear. There was just a strip of white, like smoke." He frowned, trying to find words to describe it. "Like from dry ice, you know? But it was moving, fast, snaking though the fog, pouring down the hill. I started off parallel, trying to keep up with it. Next thing I know, I'm right at the bottom of this really deep hollow. He was heading in this direction." Andy looked around. "He's got to be somewhere here. Let's try down there."

They were approaching the last part of the long avenue when Andy turned round. The pathways seemed to be orientated roughly on the points of the compass. This one led east. Andy looked up. He had not realized it was as late as this. The sun was a small red disc dropping down behind the surrounding ring of trees. The mist was coming back thick, creeping along the ground, up to their knees. He was opening his mouth to speak, when something about the expression on Ellen's face stopped him.

"This is it," she said in a low voice, almost a whisper.

They were in a dead end. Huge iron gates barred entrance to the last monument. It jutted out of the hill, a family vault of the high Victorian period, a massively built mausoleum of dull black stone. From a distance it appeared as imposing as it must have done when first constructed, but closer examination showed chunks of masonry strewn around the base. Council stickers, red letters on a white background, warned about its dangerous state. Someone had been making attempts to halt the state of near collapse. Huge wooden props held back the structure above it and corrugated iron sheets had been put across the top to cover up the holes.

Ellen was staring up at the wrought-iron work. It would have been easy to assume that the heraldic device above the archway was some kind of bird, an eagle, maybe, or even a phoenix. This was not the case. The wings, still coloured by flakes of gold and vermilion, were scaled, the tail curved and pointed. The head, turned to one side, was definitely reptilian, the jaws, open wide, spewed fire. It was a dragon. Arched above it, in rusting black letters, was the family name: SZEKELYS.

25

They stood for a moment, indecisive, then Andy transferred the hammer and chisel to his pocket.

"Come on," he said. "Let's get it over with."

The stone entrance was propped, as was the passage inside. There was no wind, the day they left was perfectly still, but the building seemed to groan and shift as they entered. A pattering of stones and falls of dust accompanied the movement.

The rooms to either side held nothing besides a litter of debris from the roof and signs of animal occupation. No human remains, just birds' nests, droppings and carcasses, the remnants of kills, or what was left of birds trapped and unable to escape. These rooms were empty, always had been, there merely for show. Whatever the building contained was underground, kept in the vault beneath.

They paused at the top of a flight of steps. It seemed colder here, water ran down the brickwork, pooling and dripping, making the stone slippery. The cold intensified as they descended. Stale air breathed up at them, carrying with it the smell of earth and clay, mixed with ancient decay. There was something else. They all felt it. A deeper chill. It seemed to sweat from the walls around them, entering the pores of their living skin, to freeze the soul and sap the will.

The stairs opened out into an archway. Andy held the torch steady. Section by section, its powerful beam revealed a long room. The roof was low, brick built and barrel-shaped. The walls were cut with shelves, double-tiered, made to bear many coffins, but there was only one. On a plinth, in the middle, was a huge black sarcophagus. Ornately carved from ebony, the wood gleamed in the light. Only the silver chasing, darkened and deeply tarnished, marked the length of time this thing had lain here.

Jenny took items from her inside pocket: slips of paper, covered in columns of Chinese characters; lengths of what looked like black twine.

"Ellen, you stay here," she said. "Keep your torch trained on us. Andy, you help me get the lid off."

"What are those for?"

"It must be near sunset," Jenny whispered back. "The papers carry powerful spells, and these threads are coated with the poison. They will stick to him, stop him from rising, while you make ready…"

Andy reached down to where the hammer and chisel weighed heavy.

A silver plate on the coffin held the dragon device. Underneath, in gothic letters, was engraved the name:

Szekelys

The lid was not fastened down but it was extremely heavy.

Bit by bit, they managed to inch it across. There was a hiss, like a vacuum released, and they both turned their heads away to avoid the smell, a combination, sickly and pungent, of animal decay and fungoid rot. It seemed to flow out towards them like some thick escaping gas.

The lid hit the ground with a hollow booming sound. Andy had been trying not to think about what they might find inside, but he had expected the coffin to be lined with silk or satin. Instead, the body was lying in what seemed to be earth, but was more like leaf-mould. Here and there shards of bone showed, white and porous, among fragments of rotted wood and discoloured cloth.

There was no movement in the chest – he lay in some state between sleep and death. Perhaps the poison had worked after all. The thing looked like Stacey, but the everyday clothes only added a note of grotesque parody to an appearance that was no longer human. His tie was neatly knotted below a face yellowed, distorted like melted wax. His hair, coarse and thick, looked like a cheap wig. The hands, extending from his suit cuffs, lay cupped, nails drawn together like claws, crossing each other, all curled up.

Jenny placed the papers at four points on his body: forehead, shoulders and the base of his abdomen. Then she wove backwards and forwards, covering the top of the coffin in a mesh of black threads.

"That should keep him secure. It will make the other work easier…"

Andy took the hammer from his pocket, placed the chisel where he thought the heart must be and prepared to strike.

In the crypt the silence was profound. Only Ellen,

standing on the steps, heard the tiny sound. A digital watch alarm. It was on Andy's wrist, but he was concentrating so hard he didn't even hear it. It was set to go off on the hour, but the watch was fast and had not been adjusted. The time was, in fact, six minutes to four. The exact moment when the sun dropped below the winter horizon.

Something stirred in the coffin. Then talons ripped through the black thread like so much cobweb.

The thing inside began to rise. It turned its head. Andy's step back was automatic, but he could move no further. He seemed subject to sudden paralysis. He could no longer feel to grip. The iron and steel fell from his hands, clanging on the stone at his feet. He stared, unable to tear his gaze away. The eyes that held his were completely red. The whites were suffused with blood, the pupils dilated; the retinas reflected light, shining ruby bright, like those of some terrible predatory animal.

There could be no escape. The sun was setting, day was waning, night coming on. The Chinese poison had been strong, and unexpected: it had weakened him, but now they had come to him, their pure young blood the perfect antidote. He let out a sound, a sigh of satisfaction. They had interfered, tried to stop him. It was fitting they should pay with their lives. They stood by, mesmerized, helpless. He had them in his power.

His lips drew back, revealing the teeth beneath. He had two ways to kill. The first was immediate and reserved for lesser creatures, like those women of the street he had slaughtered as Szekelys. The second was lingering and far more subtle, more exquisite. It was this method he intended to use here. The front incisors slicing through the flesh on the side of the neck, sharp as a scalpel. The needle-pointed canines would follow, penetrating the carotid artery like a hypodermic, allowing him to draw off the bright arterial blood.

Jenny trained all her attention upon him. Her neck ached intolerably as his smile widened and he slowly began to lever himself out of his casket. Her mind felt numb, unable to function, as though it had been anaesthetized, but some part of her registered a slight shift in the vaulting and she felt powdered brick shower down on to her head and shoulders. The stone building they were in, apparently so solid, was as fragile as an eggshell. The props on the roof above were holding up half the hillside. The wood was inferior stuff, inadequate to support the weight that it carried. Week after week, month after month, the tension inside built up until the staves were ready to snap like matchsticks.

The groan of rending wood was too small a sound to penetrate so far underground but they all heard the accompanying fall of stone, felt the vibration as it hit the floor above and shivered down the walls around them.

Damp clumps of mortar, made rotten by decades of percolating ground water, fell on to Jenny's upturned face. Starting at the far end, in a slow zig-zagging motion, the brick skin of the roof was breaking apart like a zip. She ran to Andy, grabbing his hand, pulling him towards the stairway where Ellen waited. Linked together, they leapt up the steps in a desperate race to gain the entrance before they were buried under tons of stone.

They left the building just in time. The whole hill seemed on the slide. The tombs, built into the slope in tiers, were toppling, one on to another, collapsing like a stack of dominoes.

They ran on and on, not stopping to look behind to see the extent of the destruction. They did not have to: the outward blast of cold stale air, flying stone and choking dust told them enough.

Their flight did not falter until they reached the gates, a road, street lights. Only then did they wipe the sweat from their faces and look back. Darkness had moved in, closing the cemetery off from them. It stretched away, black, impenetrable, intent on keeping its secrets. There was no sign that anything unusual had happened within its shadowy confines.

They stood for a moment, saying nothing, but each wondering if it would be enough to stop him. Or was he, even now, rising unscathed?

The building, which he had used as a haven, brought about his final destruction.

In his arrogance, he dismissed Jenny's threads as peasant superstition, powerless to affect him. He failed to notice their change at his touch. They became sticky, almost liquid. When he tried to escape from his coffin, they held him, gripping round his legs and lower torso like stretchy gum.

Held fast, he struggled, head back, trying to extricate himself. He saw the stone fall, the rusting corrugated sheets sliding inwards, the broken stave tumbling, end over end, towards him. In one clear moment, he saw it all. The stave came through the gaping hole in the roof, penetrating his chest, sharp as a javelin. A block of masonry, falling behind it, acted like a giant mallet, driving the stake home, skewering him to the ground below. He watched helpless, staring upwards as one iron sheet came down faster than the others. It descended like a guillotine, severing his head clean from his shoulders. The skull left his neck already crumbling. It blew across the floor, a shrinking pile of dust.

26

Dr Frank Stacey, formerly the Count Szekelys, was dead. Whatever power he had over the living died with him. The wound on Jenny's neck disappeared. Not merely healed; by the next day it had gone completely. There was not even a scar. Just a faint blue mark, like a line drawn in biro.

The greatest proof was Ellen herself. Her health was completely restored. She felt better than ever before. She was kept in hospital for a few days' observation, but it was as though there had never been anything wrong with her, all her test results were normal. The doctors scratched their heads; her mother thought it a miracle. Ellen knew better, but kept the secret of her recovery strictly to herself. She thought Gran might suspect something, but if she did, she never mentioned it. Neither did the others, Andy and Jenny. The shared experience tightened the bond between them, but it was too close to talk about, best kept under wraps at the moment. Each had a superstitious dread that to speak about it, to refer to it in any way, might start it up again.

There was one thing that Ellen had to do before she could go on with her own life. She had to know the rest of her great-great-grandmother's story. She went back to the metal trunk, still there under the bed, back to the other Ellen, her great-great-grandmother.

She removed the diaries and laid them out carefully. The handwriting, still clear and well-formed, became looser, more assured, losing its exact copybook precision as it chronicled an adult life. She put them in order. She would read them later.

The diaries shared trunk space with other things. Underneath were photographs, certificates. Ellen began to sift through and soon became absorbed in the lives documented by them. A wedding. Thomas Macmillan, physician, Ellen Isobel Laidlaw, spinster of this parish. Ellen Laidlaw-Macmillan, MD – certificate to practice medicine. Ellen turned these over and looked at a collection of yellowed newspaper cuttings held together with a rusty pin.

The first referred to another wedding: Miss Marie Barnes, maidservant, to Ivan Szgany, medical attendant.

Beneath that was a card: pale green, decorated art nouveau style.

Enid & Grace Wickham
Milliners – Haberdashers

With it was an advertisement, with the same lettering but bigger, grander.

WICKHAM'S DEPARTMENT STORE

It was in a northern town. Ellen wondered if it was still in business.

Then came a bundle of obituaries, dated 20th January, 1897. They had been written by eminent physicians, lamenting the passing of one of their number: Dr Anthony Laidlaw. They were all generous in their praise for his philanthropic work among the poor of the East End, and the value of his contribution to the study of the blood. His death was a bitter blow to the profession. There was a general hope that his work would not be lost, that someone would be found to carry it on.

Finally, there were a number of notebooks, their square graph-paper pages containing what looked like family histories surrounded by writing. They were obviously case studies of some kind. Ellen was just about to put them away to look at some other time when one of the notes, written in the familiar neat hand, caught her attention.

There is a definite pattern to this. Each of the women has a healthy first child, but subsequent babies are stillborn, or die at birth or soon after. The midwives know the pattern. They do not use the correct medical term, they just call them blue babies. There must be a reason. If there is, why don't we know? Why can't we cure it?

I was thinking about this last night, when I seemed to hear a voice. It was the Countess. I have not thought about her, or her cousin, or that whole strange interlude, for years, not since Father died, but I could hear her as clear as if she was in the same room. The accent, the tone – unmistakeable.

"Carrying a child interfered somehow. Maybe one blood fights another. Who knows?"

It set me thinking. It is not type, we know that. There

must be some other difference in the blood of mother and child. Like right hand, left hand. Something opposite...

Ellen stood up. Someone was calling her. She closed the notebook, sensing the importance of the moment recorded. Maybe good could come out of evil after all. It marked the beginning of Ellen Laidlaw-Macmillan's tireless search for what is known as the rhesus factor, what she termed, *"blood sinister"*.

By the time she reached the stairs, her mind was made up. Andy had asked her, the first time they went out together, "What do you want to do? In the future?" Ellen had been forced by her illness to reply, "I don't know. I don't think about it." She did, of course, but then she was used to thinking about the future like a person who didn't have one. Things had changed. Suddenly she had a whole life in front of her.

She knew the answers to his questions. There would be a lot of catching up to do, she had missed so much, but it was not impossible. She would get on with it, as soon as she got back to school. It would not be easy, there was a very long way to go, but in the end she would be a doctor. It was in her blood.

Don't miss Celia's fantastic new novel

THE
STONE
TESTAMENT

Everyone was dead. Not just in that room, but in the next, and the next. She knew because the flies told her. One or two at first, in aimless heavy flight, buzzed and banged against the windows, but the weather had been very warm, freakishly so for the time of year, and now the sound was a constant, busy, monotonous drone as if the many had become one. She could feel the imprint of their tiny clawed feet as they crawled across her face, her hands, every part of her body that was exposed, but still she did not move. Even the flicker of an eyelid would give her away. The flies did not come alone. Baal-Zebul moved with them. This was how she knew him. He had been given many titles over the millennia, but the meaning of his name was always the same: Lord of the Flies.

The destruction would be general. The Fifth Age of the World would end in fire and flood, tempest and tumult. The Beast Gods would stalk the land and only the Children of the Sixth Dawn had been forewarned. Not just here, but in identical communities all over the country, all over the world, the Children of the Sixth Dawn, C6D for short, had left early, going to another level to await the Endtime, the final setting of the sun.

She had been taken young. She did not know her age, or her true name, or the place of her birth. She had no memory of the time before they took her, but sometimes, in dreams, she saw a place that was very different from this: a place that was the colour of ashes, a land of craters and ruins where a hot wind always blew and the dust was white with stinging salts. Sometimes she saw a ruined settlement: mud huts, crumbling to dust, straggled out of a burning town. Behind them, a dried-up lake, behind that, a line of grey hills riven with black gullies. In front, lay a highway with no traffic on it. A thin dog tore and worried at a lump of something that lay beside a wreck at the roadside. She knew there were people, crouched in the corner on the mud-stamped floor of a hut half destroyed by rocket fire, but there were no people in her dreams. There were never any people in her dreams. She was always alone, tasting the bitter wind.

They had probably purchased her. When they were harvesting, they went well equipped with dollars. They went to countries which were poor to begin with, torn by war and conflict, where there was no lack of people willing to sell their children. They had given her a name: Zillah. They consulted a name book when they took in new children, working through A to Z and back again, as methodical in this as in everything else. She had no surname, no family name. She was a Truechild of the Sixth Dawn. That was seven years ago. She would have been perhaps seven or eight years old, older than their preferred age for taking children, so now she was probably fourteen or fifteen. Old enough, anyway, to be moved to the Women's House, which was where she lay now, surrounded by the only family she had ever known. She felt no sorrow or pity for the dead who lay around her. She held no affection for any one of them. Relationships of any kind had been discouraged. The children in the Kinder House were regularly rotated to discourage friendship; their carers constantly changed to prevent any kind of bonding between adult and child. All contact with the outside was, of course, strictly forbidden. To be a Child took believers beyond earthbound ties of family and friendship. Such relationships were invalid. They were formed of clay. That was what they had believed. And they had all been believers. They had obeyed the edict. Taken their lives without question. Now they were all dead and her only feelings were anger and contempt.

All love was reserved for the Divine Founder, saviour and preserver, the ineffable I AM. His was the only true religion, based on vision and visitation. The Founder had passed on to a different level years ago, but his work was carried on by another, the Advocate. All other belief was false. It was all written down in *The Meaning of the Sixth Dawn – The Book of the Law*. This was the only permitted work, but Zillah had found other books.

The Children of the Sixth Dawn had community houses, called Chapters, spread across the world, but this was the Master House. Formally called Ringmere Hall, it was perfect for the Children: a secluded mansion set in large grounds deep in the English countryside, with electronic gates at the top of a long drive and high fences all around. The main building was very grand, fashioned from dark honey-coloured stone and built around a central courtyard. The Children only used the porticoed main building and the two wings leading off it; the eastern range over the entrance was sealed off from the rest of the house. This was the Founder's Wing, where he had lived when this was his home. It was kept as he had left it, with nothing changed, in anticipation of his possible return.

Entry was forbidden to all except the Advocate.

Zillah found a way in when she was ten or eleven. A small door at the foot of a neglected flight of steps led to the sequestered wing. She'd kept her visits infrequent, choosing her times carefully: afternoons when the younger children were supposed to be resting, or in the grounds exercising; at night when everyone was sleeping. She collected stubs of the candles used in ceremonies, stole matches from the kitchen and moved like a ghost through the shuttered rooms. It was clear that the wing had not been occupied for many years. Wallpaper peeled and tapestries gaped, the heavy fabric torn by its own weight. Dark portraits glowered down from the walls and shrouded furniture made vague shapes in the dim light. The rooms smelt of coal fires, long extinguished. The corridors were swept clean but cobwebs hung like banners from the ceilings and dust lay on every other surface. Zillah was careful not to touch anything and crept from room to room, fearful that she might find the Founder's mummified form stretched out behind the drooping canopy of one of the four-poster beds, but there was no sign of him, or anyone else.

Except in one room that Zillah called the library. Books lined the walls and lay about open on tables, as if someone had just been reading them. When Zillah found this room, her heart beat harder. She stood on the threshold, gripped by fear. The small, windowless room was completely free of dust and cobwebs, which meant it *was* visited, and frequently. A leather chair was pulled up to the fire. Next to it was a small round table with an oil lamp on it, a decanter of amber liquid and a glass coated with a sweet, sticky residue. Some kind of alcohol, she guessed, although such things were against the Law. The ashes in the grate were still warm, and a large coal scuttle contained the makings of a fire. Leather trunks and suitcases lay in a row on the floor. If she was found in a forbidden area, there was no telling what would happen to her, but her curiosity overcame her. The suitcases tempted her into the room.

The battered leather cases were stamped across the corner: B. G. Wesson. A chill ran through her as she recognized the name of the Esteemed Founder before he shed his earthly persona, but she was curious. She had never thought of him as a real person with possessions. The cases were covered with old labels, half torn off, brown and brittle, from all over the world. Inside, they contained a baffling mix of things. One was full of old documents: maps and manuscripts. Another contained personal papers of some sort: curling, dog-eared letters written in the same cramped hand on small sheets of cream paper, the ink fading to sepia. Another appeared to contain bits of rock, some marked in red crayon to show where there might be an inscription. The last contained a series of small objects, their shape uncertain, worn away over time, or sucked by the sea. There was a strange, domed box, made of discoloured bone or ivory, brown and streaked, like an old man's teeth. It was covered in faint symbols, worn to mere scratches. It was empty. The inside was lined with padded green leather, ridged and gnarly, like crocodile skin. Zillah was about to close it, disappointed, when she saw something gleaming through a crack in the lining. Zilla reached in to retrieve it, using her finger and thumb like tweezers. The object was small, but made of gold. It was hard to see what it was, but Zillah thought it was a bee. The wings had broken off, the body had been smoothed by age, but there were still faint stripes on its back, and the shape tapered from a broad head to where the sting would be. It fitted exactly into the palm of her hand.

At that moment, the cobwebs in the corridor stirred and fluttered, disturbed by a draught of cold air coming from behind her. She listened and her ears seemed to move on her head as she heard the gritty scrape and tread of feet on stone. The door by which she'd entered was not the only entrance into the room. She shut the box with shaking fingers, checked that she had disturbed nothing, and crept out the way that she had come.

It was afterwards, when she was back in the dormitory, that she realized that she was still holding the golden bee. She'd never owned anything. Personal possessions were not allowed. Everything was communal, even clothes. This was the only thing she had that was different from anybody else. She had kept it ever since, making a pocket for it in the mattress of each successive bed that she occupied. Somehow, having it near her, made her feel safe. She had it now. Clutched in her hand.

The library was used by the Advocate, and only by him. Only one glass, only one comfortable chair. So she confined her visits to when he was away from the house. It was easy. He travelled extensively – tireless in his mission to take the message all over the world. They were told of his whereabouts in the announcements made at Prime, so she would know then if it was safe to go to the library. She read with a hunger. The books were strange to her because all books were banned, apart from those written by the Founder. The only one she'd heard of was the Biblos. The Holy Book. The Founder used little quotations to justify things that he said in his own writings. Now, with the whole text in front of her, Zillah could see how he had corrupted what was written, twisting the words to serve his own ends. The more she read, the more she realized that *The Meaning of the Sixth Dawn* was a crazy mass of borrowed beliefs, as flawed as a jigsaw where the pieces had been cut to fit.

She wondered how anyone could possibly believe in it, yet C6D was a worldwide movement. New Chapters were formed every day, and more and more people were wearing the multicoloured bracelets, woven from threads of brown, blue, red and gold. It was belief based on blind faith, not logic. Hope for a Better Day. The Children Will Show the Way. Slogans mixed and merged in bright, oily colours, swirling like a film on the surface of her mind. They shifted to show the truth at the heart of it. The craziness was all part of it. In the dim, dark rooms of the forbidden wing, Zillah explored rare and unusual volumes. Many were very old, with strange illustrations, written in languages she did not understand, but the sense of evil was palpable. She began to discover who they really were, and the terrifying, dark secret that lay hidden within *The Book of the Law*. Then something happened that was so far beyond her wildest, most nightmarish imaginings that her visits stopped for ever.

She had taken a wrong turning on her way into the Founder's Wing and had somehow ended up in the cellars. Attracted by a flickering purple light, she came across a small chapel, the short central nave made narrow by elaborate carving that snaked and writhed over every surface, curling round the fluted pillars and arches. The Advocate must have returned early, for he was there, standing in front of a squat stone altar, dressed in his golden robe. The violet light pulsed from a dark crystal skull in front of him. He laid his hands upon the source and the light split into rays between his fingers, playing in beams across the embossed stone ceiling. Then his whole outline had begun to blur and shimmer. As he raised his arms, the robe took on different hues and colours and seemed to solidify and stiffen into chevron patterns of rayed striations, like huge feathered wings. He seemed to expand and grow bigger, as though his human form had become engorged by something else, something differently shaped, hideous and other. He raised his head, and it seemed to be crowned by curling horns, or a pair of curving crests. The thick bulge of his neck flexed and the musculature of his back rippled with smooth, sinuous movement, like a python or anaconda. From the base of his spine, flat, bony plates seemed to broaden out, elongating and extending, tapering into something reptilian. . .

Zillah locked her fingers into the barley-sugar twists of a stone pillar, praying that it was wide enough to hide her, while all the time fearing that she might faint. She steadied herself enough to step backwards, very slowly, very carefully, one shaking leg after the other. Then she fled.

She had no reason to believe that her incursions into the Founder's Wing had ever been discovered, but what she'd seen there on that last visit made escape from the Children imperative. All her thoughts began to focus on how to get away. She was old enough now to go on "fishing expeditions" to raise funds and recruit. She'd found life outside a revelation. The streets were not filled with the drunkards and thieves that she'd been led to expect. She saw few signs that these were the End of Days. She used her time well: to watch, listen and learn. She had just begun to formulate a plan, when events decided her exit for her. They were to make ready for departure. There was no more time.

Two days ago, just before daybreak, the whole community had assembled in what was still called the Ballroom. Dressed in robes of brown and black, the colours of earth and the night sky, they had processed around the intricate maze of petallate patterns marked out on the parquet floor, painted in blue, the colour of water. A lector waited at each exit, as they did each morning, robed in red, the colour of the coming dawn. This time, instead of receiving benediction, each supplicant was given a small white capsule.

Perhaps the lectors' own eyes were already on

eternity. Certainly, they were not paying much attention as the last, most junior, members of the community filed past. It was no secret what they were about to do; there had been preparations and meditations. When the process was completed it would be posted on the Internet, for the whole world to know. But not yet. To broadcast their intention too soon would invite tiresome interference from the authorities. Theirs was not the only community, and the whole thing had to be carefully coordinated from the Master House.

Zillah palmed her pill, substituting it for another, something harmless from the Infirmary that she had folded into her sleeve. First light was showing in the long panel of windows as the lectors lined up to receive their capsules from the Advocate. She took her place near the back of the large room. From the opposite wall, the portrait of the Divine Founder looked down at them: his eyes like tarnished copper coins tucked in pockets of flesh in his pockmarked face.

The Advocate turned to address them, his golden robe turned bloody by the rising sun.

"Hear, my brothers and sisters." He stared down at them. He had always been heavy set and swarthy, but lately he had begun to bear an uncanny resemblance to the Founder. They could be father and son. "Here is your salvation." His fleshy face was shining, shining with love for them as he held up a tiny white pill between his right thumb and forefinger. He raised his hand. The heavy silk sleeve fell back. His arm was thick and muscular, covered in a spiderweb weave of fine black hairs. "Today we all attain the level above human, following the Founder to another place where the bounds of flesh and time mean nothing. There we will await the Great Cleansing and the hour of our return to a happier world."

The Advocate put the capsule into his mouth. It was seen as an act of faith and the cue for the rest of them to do the same. They swallowed a measured quantity of slow-acting poison and went obediently to their sleeping places, to wait for their eternal spirits to leave these perishable envelopes of flesh.

They died without a sound.

Zillah lay among them as if she was dead, too. She performed the Practice, a complex mixture of marshal arts and meditation, daily. This allowed her now to slow her breathing, decrease her heart rate, depress her vital functions and put her mind in another place. She'd lost any sense of real time, but judged that at least a day had passed, maybe two. Zillah had not intended to wait as long as this before making her escape, but she knew she was not the only one living and breathing. The Advocate was still here. She had heard him moving around, checking the dormitories for signs of life. He'd glided through here without a second look at her. That was on the first morning. Since then there had been no sign of him, but she had not heard him leave. She should have been shocked that he was the one still alive, but found she was not. He must have taken a harmless placebo. Sacrifice would be for others to make, not himself. Because he thought he was alone, he had revealed something of his true nature. The one she'd seen in the chapel. In the Founder's Wing. Before, she had merely been afraid. Now she was terrified.

She didn't want to risk going out of her body, but she had to do it. He might have left by a different way and she couldn't lie here for ever. She had to know.

She saw herself on the bed, looking just as if she really was dead. It gave her a cold feeling, and she was wondering how the spirit could be sensitive to physical things when she saw a movement out of the window. These rooms used to be the servants' quarters. The windows were small, the narrow panes leaded, the view further obscured by creeper, changed to its autumn colour. Down through the crimson flutter, she saw the Advocate. Just a glimpse before he disappeared out of her line of vision. He was crossing the gravel courtyard from the Founder's Wing and had swapped his robe for a suit. He had a bag with him, which he cradled close to him, as if it contained something infinitely precious, like a sleeping child. He reached down to his pocket and she heard the release of an electronic car lock. He would soon be gone. The relief left her weak. And unguarded. She was willing him to get into the car and drive away, but instead he just stood there, one hand resting on the boot lid, his head cocked to one side as if he was listening or searching in his mind for something that he had forgotten. Then he was coming back, retracing his steps, treading softly across the gravel, hardly making a sound. She took herself away from the window fast, but not fast enough. She saw him look up.

The gravel crunched hard under his determined stride. He was opening the front door and crossing the hall. He was on the stairs, taking them two at a time. He entered the Juvenile Corridor on the floor below. His progress slowed as he checked the contents of each bed, but the pause was momentary. He was back on the stairs, coming up to the Women's Quarters. She could hear his feet on the floor of the narrow corridor that led to the dormitories, the creak of the door, and everywhere the sound of the flies, getting louder and louder, rising and falling as he passed from room to room, the sound becoming more and more frenzied, until they were as loud as hornets, making ready to welcome him. . . .

She lay as still as her companions, imagining herself as a little black ball getting smaller and smaller, until she was hardly there at all, hoping she would die before he found her, or at least that he would let her die quickly.